Deer
& Other Stories

Wilderness House Press
145 Foster Street
Littleton MA 01460

http://www.wildernesshousepress.com

Wilderness House Literary Review
http://www.whlreview.com

First edition October 2009
ISBN: 978-0-578-02479-0
Library of Congress Control Number: 2009928963

Some of the stories collected here were previously published, sometimes in a slightly different form.

DEER, *American Letters & Commentary*
BLUE SKIES, *Green Mountains Review*
HELP, *WHLreview*
THE ONE, *Schuylkill Valley Journal*
ELVIS OUT OF THE MEDITATION GARDEN, *WHLreview*

Book designed by Steve Glines
Cover illustration taken from Asher Duran's *"The Beaches, 1845"*
Body text set in 12 pt. Fournier
Chapter titles set in Friz Quadrata

To Miles & Estelle
With Love

Also by Susan Tepper

poetry

BLUE EDGE
(Cervena Barva Press)

Deer
& Other Stories

Susan Tepper

Wilderness House Press

Contents

Acknowledgements

My thanks to these dear friends and colleagues for their help and support:

Simon Perchik, Gloria Mindock, Peter Krok, Anna Rabinowitz, Fran Metzman, W. R. Mayo, Katie Kehrig, Steve Almond, Doug Holder, Tim Gager, Harvey Araton, Martin Golan, Ramesh Avadhani, Valerie Polichar, Nita Noveno, Rosalie Siegel, Jeffrey Tannenbaum, Caroline Berger, Madelyn Hoffman, Ira Finkelstein, Claire Carretta, Robin Benson, Ell Miocene, Mary Kelly, Jami Brandli, and my wise and wonderful publisher Steve Glines.

Deer

M onkey lets me drive the colonel's convertible. We're spinning along Reservoir Ridge clocking eighty-five; as usual hoping for deer — herds of them to come rushing out of the woods. Whoever happens to be driving will have to show off incredible driving skills, to keep the deer from ramming the colonel's metallic-blue Pontiac. Bits of bloody deer body falling onto the white leather seats. After two entire spins around the reservoir only dry leaves have landed inside. The most deer we've ever seen on The Ridge were three: small, timid ones huddled around the ditch drinking rain water.

"Where's the colonel — Nam?" I laugh into chilly wind that's beating my hair around my face, and picture the tall colonel ordering his soldiers to kill every single Viet Cong.

"Nah. Not this time. He had to go to Fort Bragg for another colonel's wedding."

Fort Bragg! I like the sound of it. In Monkey's *southern* it sticks, rolling off his tongue like thick syrup. "Does everybody brag at Fort Bragg?"

"Only the colonel," he says.

"Hah!" I smack his leg. But Monkey's looking dead serious. He worries that the war will never be over. That in four years time, when we graduate high school, he'll have to fight in Nam. Kill VC. Even VC babies. Monkey is crazy about babies. Big Heidi says that he's the only boy in school who stops to talk to strange babies in their strollers. His mother died a long time ago. When people ask how many brothers and sisters he's got, he says: It's just me and the colonel.

Near the electrified section of the fence I take the loop on practically two wheels, flying past a huge gate plastered with red signs reading *HIGH VOLTAGE - KEEP OUT - THAT MEANS YOU!*

"That means you!" I scream.

He screams back, "That means you!"

The road straightens and I step harder on the gas.

Last night Monkey had this nightmare where he was a soldier in the colonel's platoon. The colonel kept yelling orders, then different orders; totally confusing him: Montgomery torch that hootch! Montgomery step back from that hootch! Montgomery did you hear me? I said to torch that hootch!

When Monkey woke up the bed was soaked from pee.

He taps my arm. "Stop here, I'll drive. Let's go pick up the two Heidis."

"Okay. If you want to."

I take my time slowing the car. I'm thinking that I like Big Heidi better than Little Heidi. "Where should I stop?"

"Anywhere."

"Here?"

"Here's okay."

Sorry to have to give up the wheel I take the car around another bend then drive slow along the edge of the ditch. "This could be muddy. We could get stuck here."

"It's time to switch, Leanne."

I brake hard; letting the car idle; looking at him from under my eyelashes — like girls do in movies. Right before they go-all-the-way. So far, I've only allowed Monkey to touch my breasts. A couple of times I let him try licking them. When he smacks his hand up against my crotch, I punch it away. A rumor going around homeroom is that Little Heidi went *all the way* with Billy Simone. Behind his back, Monkey calls Billy *grease monkey*! So weird. And Monkey's been giving Little Heidi these funny stares. I even told him so. And the other day after school, at FRIEND-LY'S, he let her scrape all the colored sprinkles off the top of his sundae. When she wasn't looking I whispered: "You never let me. Not one single sprinkle."

Shoving one another, we climb over the hump in the middle and switch places in the convertible.

I lean back in the seat. "You know, I think Little Heidi has to stay after to make up a science lab."

"Big Heidi, too?"

"No, she's not stupid. Just Little Heidi."

I watch to see if this pisses him off. But he just nods, and the car lunges forward leaving a dirt cloud.

"We can smoke roaches in the parking lot while we wait for her," he says.

In our entire school, Monkey is the only kid who lives on Fort Dix. Because he's out of the district the colonel has to pay shit-loads of money to send him. It's the only school for miles around with a science lab. The colonel believes that science is the wave of the future. Whenever the colonel's at home, a special green army car, driven by a soldier, takes Monkey back and forth to school. When the colonel's away, Monkey borrows the convertible. Paying the soldier off in fat joints to keep quiet.

He pulls out a roach clip made from a paper clip. "If we put the top up we can toke while we drive."

"No, thanks! I don't need you getting all horny on me while you're driving."

"Who said anything about that?"

"Then put it up. What do I care. Put the goddamn top up." Cramps are moving through my stomach like I'm about to get my period. That could be some mess on the colonel's white seat. I reach out and spin the radio dial so fast it screeches.

"Don't you just hate that MURRAY THE K dee-jay with his stupid *submarine race watching club?*" I spin the dial away from that station, keeping an eye out for any possible deer.

Monkey is stomping on the gas pedal making the car jump.

"Submarines my ass," I say. "It's just a make-out club. Cousin Brucie is a much cooler station. By the way, do they have submarines in Nam?"

"In the paddies with the water buffalos?"

"Forget it, Montgomery!"

Slapping the sun-visor down I stare into the little mirror. Because of my green sweater, my eyes look more greenish than grayish. I can't decide if I'm pretty or not. I used to think Little

Heidi was pretty, then Big Heidi.

"Don't *you* start that Montgomery stuff," he says. "First you call Little Heidi stupid, now you're the one's being stupid."

I smack the visor up, kicking off my Indian moccasins and peeling off my sweat socks, putting both bare feet against the windshield.

"Foot prints," I tell him. "If the colonel dusts the car for prints you're screwed."

We screech out of The Ridge onto Fairway Road, where old men golfers wear strange plaid pants and spend whole days whacking golf balls.

"I don't like you that much anymore," Monkey says.

I take my feet off the windshield and look at him. I'm trying to picture him old like the golfers. I can't. His baby-face is a pale circle like the *man in the moon.* Around his ears blond hair is starting to shag real nice. When the colonel gets back from Fort Bragg, and sees, for sure he'll take him to the army barber.

Last summer Monkey hid out for a couple of weeks in Big Heidi's mother's fallout shelter, built inside the potato cellar of their basement. He ate tuna straight from the cans and DOLE peaches. He slept on their emergency cot. Till his hair grew long enough to cover his scalp; till he wasn't ashamed anymore.

As we drive down the road into town I can see the maroon bakery awning flapping in the breeze.

Bouncing on the seat, I tell him, "I need an eclair. You want one?"

"Yeah. One of each. One cream, one custard."

"Custard? You hate custard."

He stretches his arm across the back of my seat, tapping along with SGT. PEPPER'S LONELY HEARTS CLUB BAND.

"How can a sergeant get lonely?" he says. "Those guys never get a second away from their men. They don't have time for any bands. This is a really stupid song."

I lean my head back until it touches his arm. "You hate custard."

"The custard one is for Little Heidi." And he slides his arm away.

My mouth drops open. "I was going to treat, but I've changed my mind."

Across from Dreesen's Bake Shop he parks in a space

under a thick tree with orange leaves. Looking up, I'm thinking: more leaves, more leaves in the car.

"Do leaves stain?" I rub the white leather seat then sniff my palm. "I mean, if you let them stay on the seats for a long time? You know, this seat smells real animal."

"I always let you drive, Leanne. You should treat for the eclairs."

I put my socks back on, then my moccasins, pushing open the heavy car door. A nice sweet smell is blowing from Dreesen's. Skipping a little I follow Monkey across the road.

"Let's first look at the fat," he says.

Through the bakery window we stare in at the doughnut machine. A tray at the bottom holds a deep pool of fat. Right now it's still golden liquid. By suppertime, after the bakery closes, we like the fat best — turned hard and solid white. We like to imagine how it tastes.

Monkey thinks it tastes sweet like HALVAH bars that are the colonel's favorite candy. I think it tastes sour like hard cottage cheese. "No such thing as hard cottage cheese," he always tells me — "it's soft. And that's that."

Inside the bakery Monkey orders three eclairs — two with whipped cream. I drop sixty cents on the counter for mine, then grab the bakery box by the string before he can.

Back in the convertible, I slide the string over and lift the lid to have a look. "I'll take the one farthest away from the custard."

"Just keep your hands off that custard one, Leanne."

I throw him a sly smile. "What if I clean my ass with my finger then give Little Heidi hers?"

"The colonel is right, you are disgusting." And he squeals out of the parking space and turns up Walnut Street toward school.

"What's that mean? Did the colonel say that? That I was disgusting — is that what the colonel said?"

It's Monkey's turn to look sly. "Maybe. Maybe."

"What is it — yes or no?"

I don't like hearing this. I don't like the colonel not liking me; it's upsetting me; I can feel cramps again. I close the lid on the bakery box and slide the string back over the top, folding my arms around it, moaning, bending toward the floor.

"I may get my period any second."

"Leanne, do you have KOTEX?"

"When I bleed, I really bleed. Practically as bad as butchered deer. This white seat will be some mess."

"You're squashing the eclairs!"

Straightening up slowly, I say, "Stains everywhere. Blobs of blood stains. It will be horrible."

Monkey cuts to the left, screeching the tires, heading up the driveway to the WAWA store. Chunks of gravel knock against the blue sides of the convertible. He slams to a stop in the yellow slashes of the *no parking* zone. His both hands squeezing the wheel; his shoulders hunched up around his ears. Staring straight ahead. "The colonel won't like that. He'll find out we've been driving. It's illegal to drive without a license. I'll be in big trouble. If I get in trouble again the colonel will send me to base school."

"Base school?"

He jerks his head. "You better check Leanne, you better look and see if your period's coming."

"How am I supposed to do that? My mother could come walking right out of WAWA. She buys her cigarettes here."

Monkey hits the steering wheel with his fist. "Well that's just great, just great."

And he turns toward me and his baby-face looks hard like a white rock. I almost jump. His face is changed into the same face as the colonel's. Only smaller; shrunken. Kind of how the colonel's looks when he's wearing his big, wide colonel hat with the *scrambled eggs* embroidered on the brim. For a second I'm almost scared of Monkey. Lowering my eyes I pluck the bakery string, listening to it slap against the box.

"Did the colonel really say I'm disgusting? Did he? Or did you make it up to get back at me for Little Heidi? Which is it? Tell me. I need to know."

"Both, Leanne."

Shoving the box at him I start to scream and tear out of the convertible. "I hate you!"

"I hate you!" he screams back.

Jumping up and down, I'm kicking at the gravel. "I hate you more than I hate my father!"

Monkey lifts the box of eclairs over his head. He pulls his one arm back and heaves it like a football. I watch it fly through the air, then it starts to sink, skids across the WAWA lot, comes to a stop in some weeds by the soda machine.

"Look what you've done!" And I'm picturing the eclairs oozing their cream and custard. Ripped apart like broken bodies. I say, "Poor Little Heidi won't be getting her eclair, now."

Monkey is drumming the window ledge with his fingers. "Who cares," he says finally.

"Yeah. Who cares."

"So I didn't know you hate your father, too."

I give the gravel another kick, swallowing down hard so I won't start to cry. "He gets drunk and pounds my mother."

Monkey is looking serious. "That's no good."

I shake my head, squatting to brush dust off the tiny turquoise beads sewed to my Indian moccasins. Then I walk around the front of the convertible and climb back in. §

String

They say keep Jesus close and you will be safe. I try doing this. Everyday I look up at his cross, and I try to see into Jesus' eyes, hoping they will give me some sign, something small just so I know he's aware of me. But they're always half shut. All I ever see when I look at him is his confusion.

***

The little blue house seemed big at first, I could spread my arms and feel the sea, each wall like a separate continent. Before Michael and me, a lady and her grown son lived in the house. Possibly forever. That's how much filth, the filth of foreverness. Mice had gone through like rain into a roofless house. Black droppings everywhere, even in among the knives and forks and spoons belonging to the lady and her son.

The minute they collected our money for the house, they just picked up, left everything behind. Even their toothbrushes remained behind in the holder.

The next day I drove there and sat on the kitchen floor and started crying. No one to help me clean the house. Not Michael. He didn't want it in the first place. He said he'd give me one month of paying double rents, one month to get it in shape before we moved in.

"Allison, you wanted it, you deal with it," he said.

Every day that month, leaving the apartment early, I went to the house. I put on rubber gloves that reached my elbows and got on my knees and scraped out wads of mouse poop with a big serving spoon from the dining room hutch belonging to the mother and son. After days of it, I bought a stiff brush from the hardware store around the corner and scrubbed inside those kitchen cabinets. Crying the whole time. It was December by then.

If I'd known about Jesus then, I would've started to pray right there on that floor. I was cold in the house. I had to keep the windows open because of the mouse smell. The reddish wood floor was so soft that when I dropped a butter knife it stuck there, leaving an indent. The kitchen was narrow but long; drifting like a vine toward the back door.

Soon after we moved in the cesspool started to seep into the basement.

"Nothing to be done," Michael said, "till the ground thaws."

He hadn't yet made up his mind whether to stay in the Army, make it his career. Because of his color blindness, or his flat feet — one or the other — he was pretty safe from being sent to Vietnam. I never got that exactly straight but what was the difference? It wasn't me who might get shipped out. Though I wanted to so badly. Ship me anywhere, I thought.

It struck me early; on our honeymoon; sitting next to Michael driving a rented car through towns with names like San Luis Obispo; a countryside where artichokes fluffed the hills.

Jesus, stay close, I pray now every chance I get.

On the honeymoon I didn't pray but stared out the window while Michael drove us in almost total silence. The radio kept at a hum. You couldn't tell which song; only that there was one and someone singing. I'd asked Michael could he make it louder. "I prefer it this way," he said.

In our new, old house there was controversy over the bedroom. I had wanted green. He insisted on gold. Gold for me would be suffocating, wheat-like, its tendrils clogging my breathing. Then one morning I would wake up dead. I prayed so hard: Please, Jesus, make it green.

It was my first direct answer. SHERWIN-WILLIAMS store near our house didn't have enough gold paint in stock, at least not the gold Michael wanted. On our way to a different paint store the car sputtered and died, had to be towed to a gas station. By that time Michael was furious, worrying about being late for the base and what his superior officer might do to retaliate.

"Get your green," he told me, "but don't make it army green."

Before he could change his mind I bought a soft winter-green color. So the bedroom would smell like mints when I woke up.

***

People kill on account of the string. You only get so much. Right at the moment of birth it's cut from your mother. Then you have to dole it out, slowly, carefully, over that period of time that is your life. If it comes off too fast you run out. Like fishing. There's just so much line.

***

Aqua for the living room and dining room that flowed together like a luscious swimming pool. Aqua, to stay afloat.

By then it was spring; cold, wet, gloomy. The windows of our house still bare. I set my portable sewing machine on the crappy dining table left behind by the mother and son. Its edges chipped like they'd been whittled with a knife.

Once, the son came back looking for his clothes. I'm sorry, I told him, I gave them away to St. Vincent de Paul box near the bank, months ago.

The clouds had just slid, making the sky a little bright. He didn't seem surprised and went off down the driveway whistling.

Every room needed curtains. But curtains were expensive unless you settled for ugly ones. Marie, my neighbor from the apartment, had the ugliest curtains I'd ever seen. When she came that first visit to our house, she urged me to buy from the same curtain outlet. What could I say?

As the weather turned warmer, Michael wanted more frequent sex. The people next door in the red house had killed a deer and left it hanging upside down in their garage to drain the blood. I had to see that deer every time I drove or walked up our pebble driveway, which ran right next to their driveway. It was impossible not to.

On the other side, the other neighbor, a skinny divorced woman, lived with her fat-bellied boyfriend. She screamed incessantly at her kids in a high pitched voice they ignored. Every few months her sister drove up in a brown ROLLS ROYCE. I wanted to get a look at the sister but she always managed to get out of the car and into the house before I got a glimpse. I did see the car, though; brown and humped as it was in front of the broken down cottage. I wondered what the rich sister thought of the fake flower arrangements in the windows?

I'd been collecting reeds, to fill baskets, from the wild overgrowth in our yard. In early spring Michael had dug a deep trench and put in piping. Now the waste escaped into the dirt like an irrigation system. I tried not to think about what was going on under there.

The neighbor with the flower arrangements suggested I grow tomato plants in the yard.

"The ground is too wobbly for tomatoes, back there," I said.

The deer neighbor offered us deer meat. I took some then gave it away to the other neighbor's fat-bellied boyfriend who was overjoyed, cooking it that same night on the barbecue.

A few weeks later my neighbor said she'd broken it off with him. "I can do better," she said.

"Of course you can," I said. But then I prayed to be forgiven of this lie. Jesus never lied. And look what happened. I stared at the sky a moment.

Michael wanted kinky sex. "I thought we already did that," I said. He wanted things with *devices*.

Oh, I didn't like the sound of it. What if it caused a permanent vibration? Then what? Jesus, help me, I prayed. Then I remembered the Virgin birth and wondered if this sort of thing was out of Jesus' area of expertise?

Michael wanted me squeaky clean. He came home one night with a douche bag. When I wouldn't use it, he steered me into the tub, pushing the nozzle inside me, pumping me full of water in the bathtub. I closed my eyes, felt myself lifting toward the ceiling.

"You're a fool," the neighbor with the deer meat told me the next day.

Our houses being so close together, I wondered if she'd looked through her window, had seen me floating near the ceiling and considered this an unsafe act. "It wasn't for that long," I said.

"My husband and sons killed that animal themselves," she said. "They stalked it through the woods for hours. It's not like it came off some supermarket shelf, you know."

"Oh, I know, it bled for a long time."

"You gave away precious venison to that slob."

I hopped from one foot to the other.

"Why are you doing that?" my neighbor said.

"I wanted to see what it feels like."

"You're extremely ungrateful." And she turned away going into her red house.

I fingered the cross I wear all the time now. The little Jesus in the middle too small for me to feel his eyes.

Michael decided we should go away on vacation. He wanted a cabin on a lake.

"Don't they have spiders?" I said. My experience with mice had sickened me to all wildlife.

He said we could pack a can of RAID.

"I want to stay here, you go without me," I said. Bring Dina, I was thinking. It would make me ecstatic for him to bring Dina. He talked of her continually: Dina this, Dina that.

"You have to come, you're my wife," he said.

Oh, no, not that.

"I just thought maybe Dina and Mark could go. They like that lake stuff," I said.

"You've never met them. How do you know what they like?"

"Well you said. You said Mark once caught a bass in Canada, and that Dina cooked it in white wine."

"Bullshit, Allison. They don't drink wine. They're in AA."

I was sure I'd heard that. I remember thinking it sounded soggy, a fish cooked in wine.

"Do you suppose they skin them before they cook them in wine?" I said.

"I told you, they don't drink."

My neighbor has removed all the flower arrangements

15

from her windows in order to clean the glass with WINDEX. In certain windows I can see her scrubbing vigorously. By the next day they're still missing.

"Where are your flowers?" I said on garbage day.

"I got sick and tired of the whole kit and caboodle," she said.

"What about your kids?"

"They went to live with my sister in Vermont."

"I meant about the flowers."

"They never noticed," she said. "So you see it doesn't matter."

My other neighbor in the red house will no longer speak to me. She refused to wave when I waved while driving up the driveway. Her husband and sons have refused to speak to me, also, turning their backs pretending to need something out of their garage.

Leftover deer meat, I was thinking picturing the extra freezer in their garage. They must be checking their extra deer meat supply, in case I slipped in some night to steal some to give to the other neighbor's boyfriend.

"They broke up!" I shouted the next time I spotted the husband outside. He still refused to look over.

It's hopeless, Jesus. And I fingered his body on the cross.

Michael I convinced to go to the lake without me. It didn't take that much persuading. My neighbor without the boyfriend told me I was living dangerously. It never occurred to me that I knew how to.

"You should dye your hair a different color," she said.

Which different color? She was non-committal saying it was just an idea; and that she'd been thinking of turning lesbian to spite the old boyfriend who had a new girlfriend.

"How will that spite him?"

"He'll worry that I'll steal her away." And my neighbor brushed a piece of hair off my cheek. "I could practice on you," she said.

Uh-oh, I was thinking; feeling my string reeling out faster than it should. She reached for my cheek again.

"No," I said.

"You only had to say *no*," my neighbor said getting in a big huff.

You see, Jesus, you see what I mean.

"Well let me know if you ever want to have coffee," she said.

"I have no problem with coffee."

"I'll be in Vermont checking on my kids."

Saturday morning Michael came home smelling of something other than fish. "You smell different," I said.

"It's the fresh lake air."

"Oh, I thought it smelled manufactured. Like from a factory."

"Allison, have you been sleeping?"

"Not that well."

"I thought so." He threw his fishing tackle down the basement stairs.

"Is that a new fishing vest?"

"Not exactly."

"I never noticed it before."

"I bought it at the lake."

"Then it is new!"

"Allison, you have to stop looking for things to worry about."

"Did you catch any fish?"

"That, too," he said.

I opened a cabinet and took out a bowl. "I'm having CORNFLAKES," I said pouring some in.

I could feel Jesus tightening around my throat when I swallowed, as if his hand were on the gold chain, yanking it up like a noose. Please don't do that, Jesus, I begged silently. But the chain was growing tighter, and I started gagging. Why would you do this, Jesus? Please don't hurt me!

I was begging and Jesus ignored me. My eyes were starting to pop, I could feel the blood in them. Then I saw that deer upside down and swinging from the rafters: all bulging eyes and frozen time.

The chain snapped. I heard Jesus hit the soft floor before actually seeing for myself.

"It only takes one bullet perfectly aimed," I said to Michael but he'd already left the room. §

Remember Hardy

That winter the army granted Hardy a short furlough to come home, though his father had died about a month earlier, around Halloween. My wife, Jen, her birthday fell on Halloween, so naturally that time period sticks in my mind.

Typical army snafu was how Hardy brushed it off; so you couldn't get a read on whether it bothered him. I had put it more bluntly. "Thanks to the army's fucked-up-ness," I told Jen, "Hardy missed his father's funeral."

It was my teaching deferment keeping me out of Vietnam. My own father, a judge, had pulled strings. Instead of facing-off with the enemy, I was sent to the inner city teaching geography to kids who didn't know that Brooklyn was a borough; never mind Vietnam. Most of them couldn't locate Southeast Asia on the map. For those kids, indifference ruled; while I had my own line of indifference— this haze that clung to my brain like a web. I'd managed to avoid going yet the place itself had absorbed me. It wasn't guilt. Nothing that magnanimous. If the deferment hadn't worked out, probably I'd have gone to live in Canada. That song about the guy who never returned, no never returned, kept playing on in my head. After a while the lyrics got scrambled. A result, I suppose, of the large amount of grass I was scoring off another temporary teacher.

Not me, no way, I used to think, watching war clips on the ten o'clock news. And, that Hardy should have planned things better.

At any rate he didn't and they drafted him; or as Hardy put it: *The army got their knobs in me.* After basic training he went on to officer candidate school. Anyone could tell they'd gotten themselves a winner. Before shipping out to Nam he married Natalie, his college sweetheart at Nebraska State.

Not even one year in-country and Hardy gets promoted to first lieutenant. At the time I had thought: *This can't be good.* Somebody else we knew had put it more succinctly: The US was losing the war big-time, the VC picking off our officers like carnival ducks and forcing these shot-gun promotions.

For his furlough, Natalie had flown in from some army base down south, while he came the long circuitous route, via Guam, on a series of military transport planes. A short visit. Too late to pay his proper respects, Jen had said.

It was cold, gray and blustery the day we all met up at the home of his family, the white cottage-style house on a bluff that overlooked Long Island Sound, where Hardy and his older brother Jack were raised. During high school Jack contracted some disease where his bones couldn't stop growing. Pictures of him healthy were everywhere in that house, and of Hardy, too, with Jack, their Mom and Dad, various dogs; even a one-legged parrot they used to call Muffin.

"I hope you like curry," Mrs. Groenfeld was saying, smiling and taking Jen by the arm and leading us into the big, square brightly lit kitchen. "You're newlyweds, right?" She directed this at Jen who was looking very nervous; also pale and thinner than usual, her nose unnaturally red and shiny.

It was then I got my first real look at Natalie. The photo booth picture Hardy had mailed me did her no justice. She was simply a pretty girl in that stiff metal-edged picture. I was unprepared for the real thing curled in a chair near the wood stove, one foot tucked under her— looking up from the book she was reading, the dark feral eyes, coal-black hair pulled back tight in a bun. This sleek as a cat, Natalie.

Wow. I couldn't help thinking it; didn't want to, but… Jen was a pretty blonde, but Natalie… when loud stomping on the staircase and Hardy bounding in, all laughs, bear hugs; his great Hardy spirit spilling over and big enough for everyone in the house. And I'd found myself thinking: It's all gonna be OK. Hardy is here now, and everything, everyone, will be OK.

"Natalie's a Russian." He was pulling her up from the chair, spinning her around wildly. "Doesn't she remind you of Anna Karenina?"

I nodded. She was laughing and dropped the book. She held out a hand to Jen, then me. When I took hold of her small white hand it felt spooky, like a skinned bird. Easily crushable. And was she really a Russian? So far she hadn't spoken, and Hardy was known for practical jokes.

"I came to this country when I was six," she said with no trace of an accent. She was peering at Jen. "You're pregnant."

Looking startled, then embarrassed, Jen said nothing in return.

"Are you?" I'd whispered. But Jen looked like she was about to cry; and Mrs. Groenfeld, who'd been over at the stove, and missed the whole thing, was calling us to the table.

The kitchen, big enough to be three kitchens, had the feel of an old-time operating room, its white rectangular tile covering the walls, long florescent tube lights suspended by metal ceiling brackets. What saved it from sterility was that bank of windows, the many small panes facing onto The Sound, a clarity that seemed to pull the outdoors in.

I took the empty seat at the table between Jen and Hardy. He was acting especially rambunctious, poking at Natalie and tickling her. I attributed this to some kind of delayed war reaction. But, then again I hadn't seen him in a few years. He was still messing with her when Mrs. Groenfeld ladled the pungent curry into soup bowls. There was also salad in a wooden bowl shaped to resemble a ship, a loaf of French bread and a new stick of butter. I poked Jen lightly with my elbow but she was ignoring me, kept her eyes focused on the table. I felt like I'd been made wrong without doing anything. I wanted to touch my wife, too; her belly in particular. If there was a child brewing I wanted to know then and there. But I also knew Jen would bolt from the table. She was the type who could be both delicate and deliberate at the same time. Instead I focused on the water peaking with white caps from strong winds and the currents off Connecticut.

Hardy learned about physical love when we were just little kids. He'd walked in on his father and mother. She happened to be one of those progressive mothers, felt the kid should *get the facts* when the kid wanted to know. Naturally he went on to tell every other kid exactly how this amazing feat was accomplished. I remember a lot of frenzied phone calls back and forth between the other mothers; my own sitting me down and telling me it wasn't true; that Mrs. Groenfeld had an active imagination.

Afterward, we talked about sex relentlessly. Me and Hardy and Jack. Out on the grassy slope in their yard that rolled down to the water. One time Hardy jumping on top of me and pinning my arms and shouting: *This is the mission position, girl, get used to it.* It became our slogan all through school: *The mission position.* We felt smug, and couldn't wait to put it to good use. Hardy did before the rest of us. He got a girl named Vickie pregnant during junior year. With all the hubbub around that, they both missed out on going to the prom. This took place shortly after Jack died. With that long painful ordeal finally over, and Hardy unable to sleep nights, he had taken to roaming the neighborhood, or swimming in The Sound weather permitting; though night swimming had been strictly prohibited by his father.

Poor Vickie got sent away; upstate somebody said; only to come back a year later, unrecognizable, her soft brown hair a brassy yellow, her breasts and buttocks filled out beyond our wildest dreams. People called her a whore. Hardy was ordered to stay away from her. But by then his tastes had changed. He was into Russian novels and wanted a beautiful Jewish girl who was on the pill.

Natalie is my soul-mate, he'd written me from college in Nebraska. *Soul-mate.* An odd-ball expression if ever there was one, I'd thought, holding the sheet of paper with his careless penmanship slopping over the lines.

That Natalie was incredible — there could be no denying. I didn't want to look at her but found my eyes kept drifting, then I'd pull them in, then they'd drift again. I didn't want Jen to see. Hardy noticed. He gave me one of his looks, the kind we'd been exchanging all our lives. At one point he said out loud, "I hear you, bro," though I hadn't been speaking.

After Jack died, he took to calling me bro. I never felt like his brother and he never felt like he was mine; we didn't talk about it; but we both knew it was bullshit. Nevertheless, *bro* remained.

It was like an old pair of pants you didn't want, but didn't toss out of laziness, or that you were used to seeing them in your closet.

"Harold likes seeds in his tea." Mrs. Groenfeld was telling this to Natalie while the two of them cleared the table, re-setting it with dessert plates and cups and saucers. "When Harold and Jack were little boys, their father worked in India for a while on an engineering project. It's a custom there to put sweet seeds in your tea," she explained. It had some meaning, but she couldn't remember exactly what.

By then Jen was at least letting me hold her hand under the table. I was thinking Hardy's mother was probably the only person on earth who persisted in calling him Harold. It had been her father's name. Early on, his dad started the *Hardy* and it stuck.

"Natalie is a ballerina." Hardy announced it with obvious pride.

Holding a cake on a pedestal cake plate, she made a gesture like she was going to smash it in his face. A good cake fight. It would've been right up his alley. But Mrs. Groenfeld had different ideas and took it away from Natalie and set it in the middle of the table. It was a high, white frothy cake covered in coconut. Then Mrs. Groenfeld placed a plastic bride and groom on the top.

"To celebrate both your weddings," she said smiling.

I was speechless. This was a celebration for her. All along I had been thinking of a wake.

Jen jumped up throwing her arms around Mrs. Groenfeld. "This is so sweet of you." Sniffling, she rested her head on the ample shoulder of the older woman.

"There, there," said Mrs. Groenfeld. "Dear, you musn't worry, you're far too young for that. Plenty of time to worry when you get older."

The next morning I went over there to give Hardy my hunting rifle, a gift from a long-departed uncle. I had never used the thing, and he had mentioned, rather obsessively, how he wanted to hunt deer, saying it was immoral that nothing was being done about the deer over-population. And why didn't the state use salt blocks for contraception? I'd thought of Vickie then, wondering what had become of her illegitimate child. Hardy's remarks contained a certain black humor but of course I couldn't say it. He went on about the deer, how he couldn't stand the thought of them starving to death over the winter. That had its own brand of black humor. In a few days time, he'd be going back to the war.

Natalie came to the door and opened it. The winds were

still gusting, I could hear soft slapping noises made by the water. She peered at me over the top of black framed eyeglasses, then smiling, as if she suddenly recalled who the person was standing there out on the porch, and saying, "Oh, Bobby." Stepping aside for me to come in the house. "I see you brought your weapon."

"Actually, it's for Hardy. He wants to hunt deer. Remember?"

She shook her head, stubbornly, as if she didn't, or else didn't want to.

"I'll go get him," she said starting toward the staircase, then coming to a halt at the bottom. She turned to face me. "I forgot, he isn't here. He went to the farmer's market with his mother."

She swiped at her forehead a couple of times as if to brush back unruly hair, but her forehead looked white and smooth. She said, "I like Jen, I like her a lot. But she doesn't like me, right?"

Standing there holding the unloaded rifle, its barrel nevertheless aimed at the ceiling, once again I was feeling unfairly singled out... for what? Persecution? First Jen, then Natalie had me on the carpet.

When we got home late I had kissed Jen's belly till she finally confessed to being pregnant. By then we were into heavy petting, and the rest that followed was wild and soft and insane. Pushing in her, I kept seeing water trickling over rocks in a stream.

Natalie had stood waiting for an answer. She was like stone. Her infinite patience came out of her like an odor.

"I'm sure she likes you. She likes everyone. Why wouldn't she like you?" Simple enough. We both knew I was lying.

She flicked at her lip with her tongue. "I can see into the future. I can see that baby, and she can't, and she wants to be the first to see her baby. I can understand that. It's every woman's dream, to see their baby first."

Actually, the doctor who has his head practically shoved in the birth canal, is who gets to see the baby first, I was thinking, almost snickering. I said, "I'm sure it's not that. What do you mean you can see into the future?"

She rubbed at her forehead again. "I saw Hardy years before we met. I saw him, then we met." She shrugged. "I don't understand it myself, I'm unable to control it, nothing like that. I have no special powers. I just see certain things ahead of when they happen."

"So you're a clairvoyant?"

Looking angry, Natalie shook her head. "I really want Jen to like me. It's important. It's vital. It's vital to us all that we like each other."

I took a few steps into the living room and placed the rifle on the brown couch. It looked funny there, like it was taking a nap. I thought about Hardy using it to kill deer and this bothered me, though I understood his intentions. Good intentions. Even as a kid he couldn't tolerate any kind of animal pain. Once some kids had cornered ants on the patio, covering them with a coffee can then banging on it with a hammer, raising the can to watch the ants stagger around like they were drunk. Hardy had grabbed the hammer. Running down the slope, he'd heaved it far out into the water.

"I think you're over reacting, Natalie."

Her name tripped nicely on my tongue. Nat-a-lee. I thought of Hardy saying it, his mouth pressed against her hair, black Russian hair damp in strands while he banged her. And I felt the envy creeping into my face.

Turning toward the door so she wouldn't get to see, I told her, "He can keep the rifle." And I walked out of the house.

Two days later he phoned to thank me.

"Did you kill a lot of deer?"

"Enough."

"What will you do with the meat? Freeze it into venison steaks?"

"I could never eat what I've killed," he said. "Natalie has this plan about the hides, something to do with selling them to a glove maker so they're not wasted. I don't know. It doesn't interest me." He sounded remote, far away, like he was already in a foreign country.

"You mean you still have them?"

"The bucks. Hanging upside down in the garage. You know, draining."

"How can you stand to look at them?"

"What do you mean? I saved their asses. They would've starved to death out there. There's no natural predators, anymore, nothing. You should see what goes on in this world, Bobby. You really have no idea." §

Blue Skies

It should have been the start of a perfect morning, Gunter awakening him early, singing that old BLUE SKIES song he always sang when the day dawned clear and bright, and they were all out there together, for the weekend, at Gunter's house in the woods of East Hampton — a crooked mile from the beach: he and Gunter, and the blond Fischl twins (Reed and Barry), and Gunter's cousin Helmut who sometimes brought his Latino boy, Louis, and sometimes a stray.

Today, however, was different. When Lenny opened his eyes to that song being sung in that same old out-of-tune way Gunter always sang it, he wasn't in the big bed watching Gunter move about the loft, stretching and flexing his long lean back, pulling his running shorts on over his tight tanned ass, ruffling his incredibly thick, wavy natural black hair. Instead that song drifted down from directly above the small room where Lenny now slept by himself. And, along with it, a stench of smoke from the French girl's GITANES cigarettes.

Chantal did not travel light. Thundering in last night, at dusk, driving a rusted yellow FIAT in need of a new muffler and a good washing. Stuffed in the back seat were two yelping poodles, one black, one white: Claude and Maxim. Not of the lap variety.

Her impending arrival announced, unexpectedly, by

27

Gunter, the weekend before; over an outdoor lunch at the Clam Shack. No mention of dogs. "What!" said Lenny, "you've invited *a woman?*"

Except for Louis who said *wow*, nobody else seemed particularly interested and they continued to eat lunch. Then Gunter asked would Lenny mind moving his things to the green room — the green room!

Lenny's mouth had dropped open. "You want *me* to sleep in the ferns? Not her?" Referring to the small, twin-bedded room with the fern-patterned sheets.

"Yeah," Gunter said. And taking a wedge of lemon he'd baptized each of his two-dozen cherry stone clams.

To differentiate among the five bedrooms in his rambling, shingled post-modern house, Gunter had assigned each stark white room a specific color scheme involving sheets and blankets. Digging his feet in the sand, Lenny did a quick rundown in his head.

The black room, really a black and white hounds tooth check, belonged to Helmut. Where Helmut went, Louis went. Easy to please, the Fischl twins had long ago settled gratefully into the gold room with the backward Nazi logo. *Grecian fretwork* was how Gunter explained that.

So — he wanted Lenny out of the loft. Out of the red satin sheets. Off the real leopard skin rug at the foot of the bed where they sometimes *did the deed.* Offering him the small green room directly below the loft, with the pair of chintzy twin beds; while the ample peach room at the corner of the house with the queen-sized bed lay vacant. Gunter wanted Lenny out of the loft. When everything between them had been so perfect. So perfect.

Positioning his elbows on the table Lenny strained forward, getting as close as possible to Gunter seated opposite him. "What about the peach room, can I take that?"

"No, Runt." Gunter almost whispered it, this favorite term of endearment, usually a private thing between them, one that Lenny savored, that Gunter cried out during their most passionate moments. It had come about due to Lenny being a very short slight man; practically half Gunter's size. Playfully, in front of the others, Gunter usually called him Jockey. Which Lenny also adored. But not the way he relished it when Gunter called him Runt.

Rather than melting him, turning his legs to rubber, bringing Lenny to his knees, he'd felt himself getting angry. He tugged on the brim of his KNICKS hat. His face burned. His gray eyes bored into Gunter.

"Why can't she take the green room?" Lenny asked.

"I want you there."

"So, she gets the peach room," Lenny said.

Gunter shook his head. No.

A silence settled over the table. Stunned, Lenny took a sip of beer. Both Fischl twins, in matching black ARMANI T-shirts, kept their eyes on the basket of steamers they were sharing. Leaning forward, Gunter slurped each raw clam directly out of its pearly shell. Pointing Louis said, "A lobster bib..." but was cut off by a rough poke from Helmut's elbow. Lenny took another sip of beer and decided that he no longer cared for the taste.

The sun had dipped behind some clouds causing the wind to pick up, carrying a chilly mist from off the ocean. Two young waitresses scrambled to collect flying napkins and paper plates and rolling plastic cups, while a line of gulls, perched like decoys on the phone wire, squalled with a sound Lenny had always linked to fun-in-the-sun, romping in the surf. Hearing it differently that afternoon — as a bleak and pathetic wail.

"Oh! Now I get it, now I get it," said Lenny. "A twin bed for a little runt of a man. Is that what you're saying?"

Helmut held up a warning finger.

Turning his chair around in the sand, Gunter sat back down facing the Montauk Highway. Lenny found himself staring at the back of Gunter's head, where his cowlick swirled revealing a tiny white sliver of scalp. Unable to believe what was happening, Lenny shook his own head. A woman. Some leather-clad cowboy would be easier to take. But a woman. Gooey, wet, disgustingly pulpy. How could Gunter?

Just hours after Chantal's arrival last night the cops had visited twice; the second time issuing a noise summons for Claude and Maxim who barked tirelessly at every bird, squirrel, chipmunk and mosquito having the misfortune to cross the *shriek dog's* path. Even the Fischl twins, normally sweetly reticent, had begun to show signs of stress: furrows appearing across their identically high biscuit-colored foreheads. Reed Fischl, the more talkative one, begging they be let off, relieved of the nightly dunk in the pool which had become a kind of magical ritual: everyone high, floating naked staring up at the stars, sharing thoughts and wishes in Gunter's gently heated azure-blue water.

"Yup, you can count me out too," Lenny said.

Despite moonlight, wine, flickering candles, dinner outdoors had been a tedious affair, choking down a vile-tasting *ter-
rine of blue fish*: an oily, under-cooked casserole the French girl
had whipped-up in the city, transporting it via the FIAT in a bat-
tered styrofoam cooler, criss-crossed with suspicious looking cuts.
Teeth marks? Canine?

Then Chantal driving Lenny mad with an endless play-
by-play of her favorite movie SLEEPLESS IN SEATTLE, all the
while shoving food into her mouth off the back of the fork (how
too too European), sucking on those stinking cigarettes she kept
lighting off the beeswax candles, tearing at her short, cropped
mouse-colored hair to make some pointless point. All in that
nauseatingly dramatic way that only French girls can do it. And
the drooling over the stars in that flick. "They were *so gweat, so
gweat.*"

How that marbles-in-the-mouth routine annoyed Lenny!
A deliberate French tactic to make them stand out from the rest of
the fumbling foreign pack. Convinced of this, he could never say it
in front of Gunter or Helmut; both of them being first-generation
German.

To kill the unbelievably bad taste of her food Lenny
downed about a gallon of Sancerre. In fact, the whole gig was
unbelievable.

All during dinner he kept watching Gunter's face for signs
of disgust. That there weren't any was even more unbelievable.
Because, he, Lenny, was totally disgusted. Burned up. Even
though *love* had never crossed either of their lips, it being more of
a long term lust thing between them. Gunter could level him with
a gaze. A gaze, and Lenny could cream. Like that! And of course
the friendship. Cheap, it all seemed now.

Dinner over, people scattered; only Gunter and the French
girl lingered at the table. Having no interest in the bar scene and
nowhere really to go except the green room, Lenny remained outdoors. But moved his chair away from the table.

Planted along the edge of the deck were fifteen blood-red
rugosa bushes; each and every one of them put in by Lenny, they
flooded the warm night air with their perfume. Taking a deep
whiff made him sad. A moan mixed with a belch escaped his lips.

Single-handedly over the years he'd dug up most of the
scrub oak on Gunter's land, replacing it with lilac, hydrangeas,
rhododendron, and those hardy rugosa roses that took so well to

sandy soil, that Gunter loved so much. Plants, apart from Gunter, being Lenny's life.

He ran his small business out of his apartment in the West Village, mainly providing offices with indoor plantings. Lately, though, he'd begun to do his fair share of roof gardens and penthouse terraces. And as for Gunter, who opened his house to them every weekend, never asking for a cent, it had been the least Lenny could do.

***

Something Chantal whispered made Gunter throw back his head and laugh. Flinging an arm across her bony shoulders he accompanied her down the wide steps of the deck, her shapeless form, in orange spandex, guiding them like a beacon onto the murky grass, where the mutts had been bounding for hours, shitting and pissing at random, destroying everything Lenny had done to make Gunter's yard a showplace.

Clapping her hands she called out, "Claude, Maxim, come here, come here you little devils."

Then Gunter shouted up that they were going to take a walk on Louse Point Beach. Yeah, thought Lenny, you do that. Let the devil-dogs crap all over the beach, too.

He found himself alone. At the far side of the pool he watched Louis, moving like a ballet dancer, encircle Helmut from behind. Insisting on kitchen duty, the Fischl twins had vanished into the house. Probably felt guilty. Guilty wasn't on Lenny's agenda. He heard the dishwasher grind into gear. He gave the wood railing a kick. Let Gunter float in the pool with *her*.

Pushing himself out of the chair, feeling like a third-wheel he joined Helmut and Louis. Tightly entwined, they were already into the first stage.

"Sorry," Lenny said.

"Hey, don't worry about it," said Louis, "it ain't like either of us is going anywhere."

"Brilliant," said Helmut untangling himself. He picked up his wine glass, the three of them staring out over the high sides of the pool enclosure.

Somewhere beyond the clearing, a stirring in the underbrush where the grass met the woods, a soft rustling: chit chit - chit chit - chit chit - chit chit.

Did the satin sheets rustle when Gunter knelt behind Lenny, planting himself inside? And they moved together as one? Lenny couldn't remember. If he'd known that he might never know, he would have paid more attention.

Out of the tree line a small doe ventured cautiously into the clearing.

"Bambi," said Lenny choking a little.

Slapping his thigh Louis laughed. "Yeah, right, Bambi."

"Where there's a Bambi, there's a sniffing buck not far behind," said Helmut. And dropped a look on his boy: *merengue-time*.

Shrill staccato barking from off in the distance sent the doe melting back into the woods. If there was a buck he was too savvy to show his colors. Suddenly very tired, Lenny pointed to a neighboring house, ablaze with lights, just a shallow acre away.

"I wonder if they're the ones who called the cops?" he said.

"Gunter always liked women," said Helmut.

"Well, I like women too," said Lenny.

"No, man," said Louis. "Gunter doesn't *mind* pussy. You couldn't do one if your life depended on it."

Lenny looked from Louis to Helmut. And he couldn't swear, it may have been the glare from the halogen spot lights, but the German cousin's green eyes looked a tinge yellow. And, amused.

"I thought you knew," Helmut said. "Men, women, women, men. Gunter likes variety. He likes change. Gotta have it."

"Wine, women and song," Louis said.

"Right," Helmut said, breezy, tossing the remains of his own wine onto the grass.

What bull-crap, thought Lenny, tempted to ask if Helmut would have chucked Gunter's cut-crystal glass into the fireplace, had it been winter. Instead Lenny said: "You call that change? I call that fucking boring. I mean, christ — SLEEPLESS IN SEATTLE."

Slipping an arm around Helmut's waist, Louis' slim hips gyrated to some inner beat. "I saw it," he said, "it wasn't so bad."

***

Cold air blasting all night long out of a vent in the wall behind the twin beds only added to Lenny's misery. At some point he'd awakened from a dream: an unfamiliar middle-aged woman, with short cropped hair and a fake hand made of styrofoam, embedded with multi-colored gemstones that kept falling off. The hand, that is.

Frozen stiff on his back under the thin green blanket, terribly, terribly, he was missing Gunter. Cradled in the strong arms, under the fluffy red comforter, cold had never been an issue. If Lenny's nose started to chill from the air conditioner, he simply lodged it into Gunter's armpit till it thawed.

Now, before he'd even opened his eyes, strains of BLUE SKIES, in Gunter's warble, floated down from the loft. Along with enough smoke from those damned French cigarettes to choke a furnace. Gunter singing to that girl was the final slam.

"Keep it to yourself!" Lenny screamed up at the ceiling.

He kicked his heels in succession against the mattress, wincing as a sharp tingling pain dug deep into his skull above his eyebrows. He rolled onto his side. Drew his knees up to his chest, covered his ears with the blanket. Too much wine, too much wine.

Naturally in all his upset he forgot to pack his IMITREX. In fact he'd packed his toilet kit, unpacked it, packing it again. Cursing Gunter the whole time and feeling strangely out-of-whack. Almost teary. With nobody to confide in. Besides. Anyone he knew would taunt him: Mary must be getting her period.

Now somewhere overhead, on Gunter's bed, or standing under the domed skylight, or pissing into Gunter's private red toilet, Chantal was laughing. Peals of laughter. Lenny stuffed his head under the pillow. He'd like to peel her all right; peel her like an onion. Layer by layer. Let Gunter see what's really inside, deep in the heart of her.

Louis was right. Lenny could never stick it in a girl, it would kill him. At least seeing Gunter with a beautiful girl would be easier to understand. The French girl was a scrawny bitch — no tits at all — the worst nipples Lenny had ever seen: brown and crisp and dry like two shelled walnuts.

Yesterday, as he watched her stroll around the pool like hot-shit, wearing just her bikini bottom, wads of hair hanging out from her armpits, Chantal scooping trail mix out of a paper bag, Lenny had wanted to yell at the top of his lungs: G-u-u-u-nter-r-r-r!

Piss, nothing else, finally forced him out of bed. Unsteady, Lenny looked down at his cold numb feet as if they belonged to somebody else. In the bathroom he did not shave or shower or brush his teeth.

33

Last night's rumpled khaki shorts, and the white T-shirt he'd slept in were good enough.

***

Under a shameless, cloud-free, china-blue sky breakfast was spread across the glass table. Everyone, except the French girl, already seated. With his head burning Lenny took the chair next to Gunter. Hating to admit that Gunter looked rested, content, confident. Incredibly sexy in a soft, putty-brown shirt printed with an exotic cream-colored raw vegetable.

"Nice design," said Lenny fingering the short sleeve. "White asparagus?" His knuckles grazed Gunter's arm; he sucked in the clean smell of Scottish oatmeal soap.

"Good guess." With that same arm Gunter reached across the table for the juice pitcher. "Actually, it's hearts of palm."

"Here, take one," said Louis, thrusting the basket of bagels at Lenny.

Cradling it against his chest Lenny said, "Ah-ha! Hearts of palm." He shook his head, let out his good-sport laugh. "I should've known that."

Smiling back at him Gunter looked more beautiful than ever. "So — it's just us guys, huh," said Lenny.

Poking through the basket of bagels he was doing his best to sound casual, while down in the grass Chantal romped with the dogs. Lenny couldn't decide. There were poppy, marble, raisin-cinnamon, onion, sesame, half a garlic. A genie could drop a bagel full of diamonds into that basket and he still couldn't decide. How could he? When all he wanted was to throw himself at Gunter, jump into his lap. Wrapping his arms around Gunter's neck, pressing his mouth to it, licking and sucking the salt out of it. Marking him with *the brand of Lenny*. That's what they all said when Gunter and Lenny pulled an all-nighter, going at it till the wee hours, and Gunter came down to breakfast a mess of welts: *the brand of Lenny*.

This morning there was no talk of it. Just bagels, and a platter of crisp sausage links, and one of eggs fried sunny-side-up that taunted Lenny like golden breasts that he wanted to smash savagely with his fork. Both Fischl twins pecked at their food like birds. But Helmut and Louis had full plates and were chowing down. Still untouched, Gunter had his usual well-done sesame bagel smeared with cream cheese and chives.

Then Helmut was saying that Gunter looked as happy as

punch, when his cousin guzzled a tall glass of mango juice.

"I am," Gunter said. "I'm one happy guy."

Against his will Lenny felt his top lip curling. He snarled. "Well lucky-fucky you." His hand shook as he raised his own glass in the air. "To your tit-less French whore."

Setting the glass down hard, Lenny picked up a fork and stabbed a burnt link sausage, shoved it part way into his mouth. "Did she take it like this?" With the sausage dangling, tears filled the sad gray eyes.

Everyone seemed to stop moving. Gunter just looked at him, not angry, not anything.

"You have sausage schmutz on your face, honey," Gunter said. He ran his finger gently across Lenny's chin, touching the grease to his own lips. "This is the best I can do for you now."

Down in the grass the poodles were riotous, Chantal laughing and throwing a ball for them.

"You see, it's my mother and this house and my inheritance," said Gunter. "And all the other neat stuff I wouldn't be able to live without." Adding quietly, "Mother wants a daughter-in-law. She wants things very respectable. You see?"

"No, I don't," said Lenny.

Hunched over he was crying openly, the platter of sausage links reminding him of dog turds, making him feel quite sick to his stomach. "You think you can do it, Gunter, but you can't. I know you. Better than anybody."

Reaching his large hand out, Gunter laid it finger to finger on top of Lenny's small one, covering it, pressing it into the table.

"I know you do, Runt. I know you do." §

Help

My wife doesn't cook. I can't remember the last time I saw her prepare more than a sandwich or a plate of cheese and crackers. We are both therapists in private practice, though I am a psychiatrist whereas Marcy is a clinical social worker. I know she comes home tired. Lord knows, I do. But there is something about entering that cold kitchen that puts me off. A stove top that never gets its share of gravy splatters, or puddles of spaghetti sauce, or any other delicious food hardened on — to leave its stain — well there's a stove top that hasn't lived a natural life. Try explaining that to Marcy, I get the hard stare, the *do it yourself* routine. Certainly I can do it myself! I don't want to. I want to come home some night to a warm kitchen where all four burners are covered by pots and pans that simmer and sizzle. I want a loaded oven. 400 degrees.

Roasting succulent meat surrounded by cut-up potatoes and carrots and pearl onions and diced celery and, perhaps, a handful of mushrooms. I want kitchen windows steamed over from so much food cooking. That's what I want.

Today in a phone conversation with a colleague, I found out that Karen Caruso, and her husband, Rick, have left the area to move to the Jersey shore. Until recently, Karen was a patient of mine. A patient for nearly two years. Gorgeous woman, total knock-out, incredible body. Also an incredibly controlling bitch but the type that did it softly — crept up on you. Before Karen, Rick had also been my patient for a short time. Rick wanted the PROZAC, I only saw him once a month. Karen was a regular.

Before going into the house, I stop a moment at the bottom of the back stairs. The black sky is a wash of gray clouds, all of it starting to break up as snow begins falling again.

Groaning and thinking *no more snow,* I climb the slippery wooden stairs, crossing the frozen straw welcome mat and entering through the mud room behind the kitchen. Still stunned by this latest news of Karen, I mutter, "Can't believe it."

Karen is a poet, she needs to live within a reasonable commute to the city, needs the life of letters at her feet. How will she survive down there with all that sand?

Shaking my head I pass through our lifeless kitchen, coming to a halt under the archway.

My wife is standing at the hall mirror fixing her short black hair. Suddenly I wish to remain mute. What must it be like to have your tongue cut off — to never have to speak again? My eyes skim the toast-colored wall, fastening onto a long crack in the plaster. It appears to be deepening. I can picture the wall breaking open, exposing the framework and plaster and lathe of the old house. You never know what you'll find inside an old wall. Years ago, while living in the city, a wall had to be opened for electrical work. As the contractor sawed into it, hundreds of thousands of cockroaches poured out.

Musing aloud I say, "Don't expect roaches." At the same time an upstairs toilet starts to flush without anyone using it.

Marcy says into the mirror, "What's this about roaches?"

And I'm thinking: *run down, run down.* Our old farm-style house is running down. A feeling of neglect, a barren quality permeates the drafty rooms, though they are fully furnished, mostly in the oranges and earth-tones popular during the eighties. The place hasn't been updated since. But neither of us ever discuss any needed repairs.

"What roaches?" she repeats frowning into the mirror.

"Nothing." I blow on my cold fingers. Marcy has brought snow in on her boots, there's a small puddle where she stands.

All summer long Karen Caruso sauntered into my office

wearing strappy sandals, her toenails painted a blazing red — it took willpower not to gawk.

Marcy turns to face me, her round eyes darkly bright under dim hall lighting. I almost say: You have exceptionally large eyes. Too large. Swallowing the impulse, I tilt my head and grin. To see my wife sparkle this way chokes me with a taste I don't care to identify. Marcy flashes her sweetly savage smile, saying, "So what'll it be, Luigi's or Chinese food?"

Luigi's! *Shit!* Italian like Karen Caruso. I grit my teeth, jiggling some change in my pocket. That's right, Marcy, rub my face in my weaknesses. Then shrugging, as if to say Luigi's or Chinese — it's of little consequence — I tell her, "You're standing in a puddle."

Lifting her boots in an exaggerated manner Marcy side steps the puddle answering for both of us. "Luigi's."

"Luigi's it will be." And I press my hands together in mock-prayer-mode and bow my head solemnly — half teasing, half shtick: the way I used to with Karen; standing just inside the doorway to my office, silently wishing her welcome: Welcome to my *salum sancturum.*

After my clownish behavior made Karen giggle that first time, I did it again and again, shamelessly, week after week. Anticipating her girlish giggle, delighting in it.

Marcy doesn't giggle but turns back to the mirror giving her hair a final smoothing. It's dyed coal-black to cover the gray. Not natural-looking; but that's not for me to say. Karen Caruso, I'm sure, dyes her hair as well. Karen is also close to fifty though she barely looks forty, and in soft lighting can pass for thirty-five. Her straight auburn hair cascades onto her shoulders like a teenager. On sunny days, if she happened to take the settee tucked under the window in my office, as opposed to one of the free-standing chairs, I'd watch the light play off her shimmering hair.

***

People just naturally expect you to start with their childhood. They like that. They want you to know about every time they spit up their PABLUM. Horse shit! You start with the *here and now* and to hell with Freud! Karen was torn up about Rick — should she stay, should she leave him? She'd tied him to the stake, and she alone held the lighted match — all because of one unfaithful foray on his part. Poor Rick. It got so I couldn't stand that perennial ping pong game Karen was playing with herself: ping and pong, back and forth, ping and pong.

Finally, after months of this, I had to lay it on her. Folding my hands in my lap I had looked her square in the eye: There is no reality, I said.

Well! You'd have thought I told the Pope there is no Jesus Christ the way she carried on, dissecting it, week after week, trying to put a firm foundation around something that could possibly, just possibly, not exist. Karen playing ping pong again. For a lapsed Catholic she had bought in to a lot of the jargon. Fascinating! I watched her disbelief of her belief system waver, take form, waver, then go totally haywire — like I'd taken a mallet and smashed the chalice of holy wafers.

Each time she made a point she sort of sprung forward in the chair – like she was about to jump out of it. Or out of her skin. Karen practically hand-wringing, so deep was her despair. *Of course there's a reality,* she kept insisting; suspicion only making her all the more seductive.

On more than one occasion she'd pointed menacingly in my direction demanding to know: If you're over there, Doctor, and I'm here, how can there be no reality? How? How?

Ah-ha! *Darling,* I wanted to say. *Darling Darling Darling.* I wanted to soothe her, bow her head to my shoulder, stroke her silken hair, drop to my knees and murmur into her belly. Instead, I smiled. Slightly. Deliberately keeping it small; saying the word almost in a whisper: *If.*

Karen, being Karen, charged right back at me.

If, I repeated even more softly. *If* is the operative word.

Ready to blow she had screamed: That's so fucked up!

At last showing her true colors. If I were a painter (that *if* again) I would paint Karen using a predominance of red. Naturally her rage couldn't be contained — she's Italian and therefore predisposed. Genetics. Quite remarkable. And after the long stretch of calm between us, it was exhilarating to ruffle the surface of her lake. And, very sexy.

Marcy has thrown off her wool coat, she's taking her down-filled coat out of the hall closet and handing it over to me.

Our long standing custom. I help her into it, sliding it up over her shoulders. At the nape of her neck a tiny black tail of S-shaped hair snakes out from the clean line of sheared bottom hair.

Disturbing. I take a step back, saying, "Have you ever considered letting your hair grow?"

From deep in her throat comes a laugh that's almost indiscernible; but enough so I know to drop the topic. Marcy slaps her gloves against the hall table. "I don't know, this coat might be too heavy, maybe I should switch back to my wool."

"You'll be fine." Anxious to get the hell out of the house, anxious to have my dinner, I sniff the air for food smells, naturally finding none.

At Luigi's Trattoria we order a soup, a salad, a pasta tagliarini — all to share. Not because we can't afford to each have our own, but because I am conscious of my weight. I want to maintain my current fighting-weight of one-hundred-sixty-nine pounds. And because Marcy has put on nearly thirty pounds this year. I'm hoping the half-portions will incentify her to reduce. She blames it on the estrogen but I'm not so sure. I watch her blowing on the spoon of hot minestrone, looking flushed and giddy as it glides into her mouth.

How in the name of Moses does Karen Caruso manage to stay so svelte? Certainly not from too much sex — sex, or a lack thereof, being the crux of her marriage problem.

Ravenous, I break off a hunk of Italian bread, mashing it into the saucer of olive oil, taking a big bite. Early on — it may have been her first session — in a rush of tears Karen announced that her marriage was dying from a lack of sex. Surprise!

I laugh, choking a little on the bread. Marcy looks up from her soup and smiles.

"Dear," I say, tapping my front tooth, "there's a smidgen of lipstick..."

"Shucks," she says, grinning wider.

And in spite of everything I throw back my head and laugh. "Oh, Marcy." But I'm thinking *Karen*. Oh, oh, Karen.

***

I know what my wife feels like. I know what she smells like. That's the thing about marriage — after a while, no surprises. I could be held hostage in some foreign country, half-starved with my eyes gouged out, rags stuffed in my ears, and I could pick out my wife — hands down. This depresses me.

I push aside the plate containing the uneaten portion of my half of the salad. There were times Karen Caruso came into my office I could swear I smelled food clinging to her. Spiced garlicky food, sauced food, delicious Italian food — the kind you want to roll around in while you're eating. An aberration — those food smells had to be. Karen always arrived for her session looking pristine.

I stab some tagliarini and twist it around the fork and shove it in my mouth. Tonight Luigi's food tastes flat.

As I'm signing the credit card receipt I ask Marcy: "What did you think of the pasta?"

"Wonderful."

***

On the average we have sex twice a week. Not bad for a couple edging toward fifty, with two grown daughters and a son, a couple who have cohabitated for most of their adult lives. Marcy keeps herself open to me, though three babies and time have stretched her considerably. I can be in there, and feel lost. Lost in space. A single molecule pushing through a dark and limitless universe.

Karen Caruso told me that her body had closed to her husband, Rick. That she'd become like a virgin again. At the time I found myself silently humming that LIKE A VIRGIN song — Madonna being the last of the pop artists to get into my unconscious; and, then, only because she was a favorite of our younger daughter, Shelley; who around that time had moved back home for a while, moving out again the same week Karen Caruso left therapy. I miss my daughter. Both my daughters.

Karen had brought up sex pretty early in the game. Almost eager, I'd say, to discuss her unwillingness to have intercourse with the unfaithful Rick. If ever a guy picked the wrong woman to cheat on! A lousy *one-night-stand*, but Karen obsessed over it, as she obsessed over the question of reality, as she obsessed over her newly acquired virgin status. Totally aware that she was making it extremely difficult for Rick to get inside her, and despite her intense suffering over it, she was getting off on it. No question.

For Rick to enter me, was how she so primly put it. Across from her, I could hardly keep a straight face. And there she sat — so damned gorgeous. And all I could picture was Karen flat out naked taking it every which way. For chrissakes, I had wanted to yell, let your husband fuck you!

That she alone was making it practically all out impossible for them to have intercourse alternately disturbed her and didn't. Her split reaction concerned me. Yet it elated me! Karen as a virgin! Something men my age don't normally experience in the course of meeting adult women. An offering from the gods!

Half-heartedly, I tried to convince her to take WELL-BUTRIN but Karen was dead set against taking drugs. And, I'll admit, in her particular case drugs worried me also. But only on the one score — that she would gain weight. I wanted Karen coming to me reed thin and beautiful.

She did. Summer's extreme heat and humidity seemed to call up her more unadulterated side. She arrived in skimpy shorts that were often flesh-colored, blending with her lanky legs which she crossed and uncrossed, restless as a colt. To not stare was difficult. The nipples of her compact breasts pushed against tight, pastel tee-shirts while Karen continued to talk about her body as a virgin body. How she wanted Rick yet couldn't stand the thought of him inside her.

Then around mid-summer she brought more news. News of another man — some lawyer Rick had consulted on a business deal, who had shown more than a passing interest in her (why not!) and to whom Karen had reciprocated this interest; letting the guy know he stood more than a fair chance.

As that information spun out of her she looked coy and animated. I had to rein myself in tight. It was one thing to have Karen with Rick; Karen with her husband was one thing. That I could deal with. But Karen with a new man — I forced my face to remain blank despite the upheaval going on inside, the tidal wave in my chest.

I tried talking her out of the lawyer but Karen was operating more out of her ego than ever. She had built up this fantasy of an incredible life once she extricated herself from the unfaithful Rick. And, so on.

Wagging a finger I had told her: Pride and anger are two of the *seven deadly sins*. Pretty transparent stuff. She saw right through me and she looked pissed. I winked trying to make a joke of it, saying: Anger is also known as wrath — you know, like THE GRAPES OF WRATH. Another pathetic attempt to appeal to her artistic nature. The whole thing fell flat.

A month went by, Karen continuing the ping pong game in her head. With the lawyer occupying her mind it was three-way:

ping-pong-ping. Ambivalence driving her. She was split. But I don't like labels. Even now — now that Karen has left me, I will not classify her schizophrenic.

***

Back home from Luigi's, in bed, Marcy presses against me from behind. I beg off, telling her, "The pasta is burning a hole in my stomach." I can feel her body go tense against me.

"You said the pasta tasted flat."

"It did. It did taste flat. But they must've snuck in some spice that doesn't agree with me."

I have to turn around now and face my wife or risk being exposed. When she's feeling threatened Marcy will tell you the truth. Tonight I'm not in the mood to be called a liar.

Flipping onto my side, yawning, I tickle her stomach playfully through the pink nightgown. I can feel her bloat. Once again Marcy feels pregnant but there's no nostalgia involved. Her belly is the round of the moon — I've touched it and been burned by its heat.

I say, "Well how do *you* feel?" This comes out weak-sounding, what I didn't want to happen.

She purses her lips. They look chapped.

"Okay," she says. "Whatever it is that's going on with you."

"A break here, please! Can you give a guy a little break tonight!"

***

Every morning I have my coffee out. I drive a couple of miles past the spread of open land belonging to the community college, past the next big tract at the school for the deaf, then up and down a grid of tree lined roads that lead me into the small, town center.

KIRBY'S is a counter arrangement with coffee and dough-nuts and plastic-wrapped muffins — no big deal. Probably I should have my breakfast at the diner, something hot and substantial like oatmeal, or a poached egg. However I don't trust myself at the diner. Undoubtedly I'd order eggs-over-easy, sausage, hash browns, a toasted bagel and shmear. Washing the whole thing down with a pot of black coffee. Never mind poundage — I'd be dead in a year!

Mornings at the counter it's mostly the same people that gather, including three men and a woman who seem to know each other well. One of the guys is a postal worker. The other two men dress in paint-splattered clothes. The woman, Babs, is curly-blondish, middle-aged and dumpy. Babs wears nylon running suits in deep shades — today's is a savory, eggplant purple that glistens unpleasantly under the florescent lighting. The four of them spend a good deal of time bantering, though occasionally something of merit pops into their conversation. As for me, they simply nod and go about their business. I'm never encouraged to join in.

I take a stool at one end leaving a few empties between myself and the guy called Dan. Dan's complaining about his wife, telling the others that they argue continually about every small matter. Because the luncheonette is chilly I'm keeping my jacket buttoned, sipping black coffee that the waitress knows by heart and pours automatically. A small thing — yet it endears her to me, this automatic giving of sustenance. Hunched over the counter I give her a grateful nod. In my woolly brown jacket I'm feeling like a bear. A bear who stands on its hind legs and must forage for its food. Thank god the coffee is starting to heat me up. I yank at the buttons on my jacket tearing it open. But that doesn't do it, I'm too warm now, I want to tear off my shirt as well, I want to stand like this in front of Karen, upright like a hungry bear — my chest exposed in all its hairy glory. *Look at me*, I want to tell her in bear lingo — *look at my chest, which I offer to you.*

Hunkering down even further over the counter I'm thinking: Boy if Marcy could hear this she'd say I've flipped.

Raising his voice, the postal worker says to Dan, "You love your wife?"

"Yeah?"

Dan's *yeah* sounds more like a question to me.

"Why do you fight with her?" asks the postal worker. "If you love her, just say yes!"

The two men stare each other down a moment. Dan is scratching his chin. "You mean I should just give in to her demands?"

45

"If you love her," the other man says. "And you want to keep the peace. It's the only way."

Bravo I'm thinking, wishing I could clap to the sad truth of it. *Bravo.*

But Dan's not so sure. Neither is the third man, Paulo.

Babs, however, is greatly in favor and pounds on the counter saying, "That's what I call using your noggin!"

Marcy flits across my mind. Marcy. Basically undemanding. Practically an angel. All the years the kids were growing up, I screamed and hollered through the house, while Marcy kept them in line with rational sweetness.

And Karen — the biggest total ball-buster ever to cross my threshold. Karen Caruso. I slump on my elbow saying, "There it is."

"Huh?" Babs shoots me a quizzical look. The first time any of them has made an overture, though five mornings a week I inhabit a stool at that counter, a few feet from them. My clothes certainly don't give me away as a *shrink* — Marcy commenting more than once on my rather unconventional (translation sloppy) clothing for a psychiatrist. For a *doctor* Marcy says, putting a bit of a snobby twist on it. She is prideful of the fact that I am a doctor, though she'd like me to look more the part. Whatever the hell that might be.

I know she compares me to our son, Marshall, twenty-five now and living on his own. Marshall dresses in expensive sports wear, and recently bought himself a vintage MERCEDES. Because of my oldish clothes, and the fact that I drive a BUICK purchased a decade ago, our son worries that I'm secretly strapped for cash. Recently offering to lend me some. I was touched. Remembering brings tears to my eyes. I was so touched. And because of that I was tempted to accept.

I place my lips around the rim of the coffee cup so as to suck the coffee down into my stomach in one steady stream. Doing this requires the most minute intake of air. I'm imagining people being force fed, a strange appeal to the idea; though my mind is telling me otherwise.

What would Karen think of Marshall? My son, with his young handsome face, strong athletic body, cool clothes and classy car? Would he turn her on? Marshall is an architect drawn to beauty in all its forms — Karen would be right up his alley. This makes me feel old; tired. I catch my reflection in the window of the pie case, and through cloudy glass see a pinched-face man with jowls; a hang-dog expression. A hungry-looking man. What man isn't?

***

Right away, right from the beginning, I knew. Coming in from out of the cold (literally), I stepped into our common waiting room that smells of camphor to keep down the mice, picked up my pile of mail from the table and there she was. Karen. The only patient in the waiting room. Technically she could have been for Jerry or Saul, or Ella Whitby. I knew she was for me — my new patient. I remember thinking: Here is a woman whose effect will be everlasting.

Forcing myself up off the stool, I pay for my four cups of coffee then head outside, shielding my eyes against strong glare. Giant snow mounds, pushed by the plows, have made a backdrop of white mountains in the parking lot. Almost painful. I squint into the distance, toward a stand of spruce, curving and green, as if hugging the low buildings. And I'm trying to figure out which way *south* is — based on where the highway dumps into town. *South* — where Karen has fled.

Choking on too much saliva I climb into the car. "I was fair to her."

The Buick starts up easily. "No reason to dump it for a newer model," I say. Who am I trying to convince? Myself or my son? When suddenly I picture Marcy and Karen in a face-off: the old model and the new. And I shudder, the car moving forward on icy pavement.

The days... the days have become tedious again. Nobody wants psychotherapy anymore. Ninety-nine percent of patients come strictly for the drugs — I've got a closet full — the drug reps keeping me well stocked. I give out samples and if it's tolerated I'll phone in a prescription. Easy. Easy work.

"Too easy," I say, veering onto the main road.

Thursday was her day. Every Thursday. And Karen enjoyed talking about her life. Even the worst of it. And I enjoyed listening to it spill out of her — all that cream. I told her: *Pearls. You bring me pearls.* And watched her flush with pleasure.

Out of habit, every few seconds I glance through my rear-view mirror. Habits being hard to break. Marriage is a habit for most people. People want to get out of their marriage, now there's a nifty habit that's hard to break. A lot can't do it. Miserable together seems to beat out miserable alone.

Behind me, the town is receding. As seen through the rear-view mirror, it grows smaller and smaller till it ceases to be. I pass by acres of white pasture fencing that hold back snow fields sparkling under winter sunlight.

There was a time, not long ago, when such scenery could lift my spirits practically to the level of nirvana. Corny, but true. Before Karen — No! No, that isn't entirely true! Before Karen *left*, before she left me, a bright clear day, the quietude of empty fields, the solitude — all of it fostered a kinship with the living and non-living. And I would go to my work feeling a sense of peace and harmony. Convinced, however stupid or erroneous, that all was right with the world. All was right.

Rarely did her husband Rick tell her she was beautiful. Karen stuck by him, though. Threatened to leave him, session after session, then stuck by him. While, I, on the other hand, told her she was beautiful. Told her at every imaginable turn.

It got so that I would look for places to insert those words — and it got so that she waited to hear. Hungry for them. Her lovely ass wedded to the chair, straining herself toward me, unconsciously flicking her tongue, wetting her lips, Karen hungry for those words. Hungry to hear them coming out of my mouth.

The moment her sessions were over, the door closed firmly behind her, I needed to masturbate, before I could see my next patient.

Then toward the end of summer Karen arrived with more news. She had told Rick that it was over between them. And he had some kind of seizure, or stroke, she said, after starving himself for a couple of days plus loading up on tranquilizers and whatever. Apparently he'd fallen down unconscious. She had tried to revive him using *mouth-to-mouth*. An ambulance was called. It was then, she said, that everything became clear. She had prayed for his recovery, prayed harder than she ever prayed in her life. She loved him, she said. Despite everything, she loved him deeply.

Absorbing all this, I had sat back in my chair watching the color rise in her face. Heat. Moving under the flawless skin.

Her sexuality toward her husband reawakened. The way he had reawakened from his unconscious state.

Then almost in a whisper I'd told her: *And you hate him, too.*

Maneuvering the car around a sharp bend in the road I'm thinking *Da Vinci.* That fevered, ecstatic expression on Karen's face as only Da Vinci could. I can see her in a painting by Da Vinci — *Karen The Immortal One.*

***

Our last session, in late September, our very last, she arrived swathed in pink. Some kind of pink top. The afternoon had been damp and gray, and the pink top covered her arms and had this soft hood into which her long hair tumbled. Karen chose a chair across from me. As she lowered herself into it, the pink seemed to stream into her face. Different from that fevered color her face took on the day she talked about loving her husband again.

Quite frankly she took my breath away. It had been over a month since we'd met. First I was off on vacation, then Karen didn't come for a couple of weeks for unspecified reasons (she wasn't telling). And knowing full well that I shouldn't, but throwing caution to the wind, I told her: *I've missed you.*

Karen looked blank. I persisted saying: *That's very beautiful.* Motioning at her top and saying, *That pink top you're wearing, what's it called?* She had kept silent; expressionless. Though I thought I detected a glimmer of annoyance.

Or, arrogance?

Switching on the heater in the Buick I'm thinking: A woman like that — a woman like that should be well fucked. Case closed. And her case is closed. I have closed the file on Karen Caruso forever.

I reach down adjusting my erection to a more comfortable position in my pants. My wife is being cheated. Cheated out of her needs. Unfair. It can't be helped. I can't help everyone. One of the first things I learned as a doctor was perspective.

"Lose that and you're a goner," I say out loud, my breath steaming in the cold car.

And I picture Marcy some night sticking the cold barrel of a gun against my forehead while I pretend to sleep.

"Christ!" And I raise the heater as high as it will go.

My office is less than a mile down the road and over the ridge. At the last minute I detour onto Pond Road, stopping the car, scanning the pond for skaters. A few geese trail its banks;

49

otherwise the pond is deserted.

"Too early for skaters," I say. And Karen. Too early. Karen has left me much too early. Blasting the horn, I watch the geese scatter, too.

I don't know about love, anymore. Over the years I've heard it bandied about so many times by so many people. All this talk about love — a lack of love, too much love, the search for love, the disappearance of love, the misunderstanding of love. I pound the steering wheel then rest my head in my arms. Love and all its myriad complexities. The mystery of love.

Did I love Karen Caruso? I don't know. About love, I can only say this: I do not know.

Sure there were some slip-ups. I may have made some mistakes. Once, when she said that she wanted to talk about sex, I shot right back with: Sex between you and me? Straight ejaculation — the way it shot out of me. And, truthfully, I was only half sorry.

Acting nonchalant Karen had answered: Sex between me and Rick.

I might have thanked her for saving me, but of course I couldn't. Probably I was too candid with her. I probably shouldn't have mentioned that mafia princess who'd been my patient. The one who still owes me money. Quite a lot of money. Forgetting myself, I blurted out how I planned on going to the girl's father if she didn't cough up the cash. I said: He'll beat her, he'll beat that money out of her. In retrospect, I probably shouldn't have mentioned it.

Lifting my head off the steering wheel, I maneuver the car back to the main road. Probably I shouldn't have mentioned that girl at the mall. That blonde kid — all of thirteen. Younger, maybe. Talk about virgins! Perfection! Untouched-looking, that girl. I suppose I was trying to make Karen jealous. Testing her; at the same time testing myself.

Both of us, we're up for grabs, I was trying to convey to Karen. What are your limits? Do they match mine?

Probably I shouldn't have mentioned how I was tempted to follow the girl, follow her through the mall.

Karen just laughed!

I told her: But I stopped myself, I didn't follow the girl, I have daughters! Two daughters.

Karen went on laughing.

What was so damned funny? That I wanted to follow the girl? Or that I lost my nerve? Or that I have daughters? Daughters — the last temptation of Christ. No matter what the Catholics have to say.

Up ahead the road is clear with sunlight streaming in shafts that seem to pierce the blacktop surface.

Almost at my office, the last moment I swing the wheel and take the turn off to the left. A pebble road leading to the reservoir, where poachers slip behind protective fencing to shoot deer. Nobody minds anymore. The deer having taken over yards and gardens, spreading their lousy disease. People today hardly remember BAMBI. I feel this truth in the pit of my stomach. Karen Caruso would remember BAMBI. It's the sort of thing a poet remembers. Once she brought a few poems to the session — luscious poems that she left for me to keep. Poems I devoured like food.

"I can't help you," I say into the empty car. Tears well in my eyes. "I can't help anyone."

Driving the pebble road I lean on the gas, bearing down, rock crunching under my tires — an altogether satisfying sound. Then stepping harder, I aim for a tall and substantial tree. §

The Grass Eye

That summer they sent for him to live in Italy the trains didn't run more times than they did. Most mornings, Teddy's grandparents (doddering, gray-haired *expats*) shuffled off to the train toting straw shopping baskets, often returning to the villa an hour or so later; disappointed. Baskets empty. Saying, "The Italians have struck again." Meaning the trains were on strike.

Something in their disillusionment, the sour expressions under the floppy fishing hats they wore, suggested otherwise. The Italians had struck again.

Living in Italy Teddy missed having other boys like Cyrus and Billy to play war with, chucking dirt-ball grenades back and forth, screaming *kill the Vietcong*! in the excavation site behind Teddy's house on Long Island.

Besides that he missed playing war, Teddy missed his old room. His collection of felt baseball pennants tacked to the walls. The villa had walls of marble. Nothing could be tacked on them. But most of all the things Teddy missed, he missed his yellow canary, Bud. Quarantined by Italian immigration.

Poor Bud, he thought whenever he took the time to notice a bird flying past. Grandpop said he shouldn't worry, that Bud wouldn't even notice since he was used to being shut up in his cage all the time. And Teddy would feel his chest tighten, remembering how the canary had gotten used to his afternoon flying time, zooming room to room, while Teddy's mother lay zoned on the couch on Thorazine.

Now Bud was locked in quarantine and his mother was locked in a mental ward. He didn't miss her all that much. Grandpop and Nana hardly mentioned her, and when at all, in whispers. Only Rosina, a girl they called their *sporadic Italian cook*, only she had something to say about his mother — *pazzo pazzo* — twirling a finger next to her head. A long time ago he figured that out for himself, so Rosina saying it was no big emergency; his mother being the reason they sent for him. Not because they were anxious to share their leased Italian villa — a big old beat-up house in a weedy garden. The walls and floors of grayish marble where grit got stuck in the cracks. Teddy scraping it out with his fingers when he had nothing else to do. The other day he discovered a family of cockroaches living inside an especially curvy crack in the dining room wall.

The marble floors were better, he liked how they dipped and swayed into hills and valleys, forming pools when the roof leaked. Before Teddy came there to live, Nana had slipped fracturing her hip while making the bed during a rain storm. She walked with a limp now, grouchy when the place began to fill up with too much water.

He paid no attention to Nana. He liked when it rained hard. He took off his shoes and socks and waded in the marble puddles; making believe he was back home with Cyrus and Billy, scouting girls at the pool in Massapequa.

So the trains were on strike all the time, so big deal. The trains didn't interest him. Neither did the lousy outdoor food market. After he went there once, Teddy decided never again. Half-alive eels and piled up fruit might turn his grandparents on; but he had different ideas.

He took to exploring the hills, hanging around the dry creek that snaked behind the olive farm Grandpop called *Verdi Mista*. It was there, on that creek slope, with the hot sun beating into his back like noise, that Teddy began burying things.

First, one of Bud's yellow feathers. When the Customs Inspector said he should wish Bud *arrivederci*, that Teddy wouldn't be seeing the canary for a long time, he stood still listening to the roar of planes coming and going. Then he plucked out a feather while that inspector was making a big deal over rubber-stamping his visa.

Later that summer, kicking rocks along the creek bed, it occurred to him to bury the feather he'd been carrying around in his pocket.

Teddy searched till he found a rock pointed like a spear, used it to make a hole in the packed dirt. Gently dropping the feather in. It seemed to float above the hole a moment, like it wasn't sure; as if it wanted to lift up into the sky and never return. Teddy had squatted there a while. The feather looked nice. Very clean and soft. Then he knew he wouldn't be seeing Bud ever again. He didn't trust those Customs guys to feed Bud the right food.

During supper a few nights later, Grandpop mentioned the villa down the road, calling it: "The one next in line." Saying it had been leased by a German family called Tolle, and that the Tolle's had three children — according to the local barber anyway (Grandpop saying that part with a wink). One kid supposedly a boy close to Teddy's age.

He was skeptical. He stabbed his fork into the first course — cold spaghetti coated with oil and chunks of garlic, flecks of green. Cooked and served by Rosina who'd pinned a dish towel to cover her dark, tight skirt. She wasn't very old. Maybe sixteen; or eighteen, Teddy decided. She spoke very little English. But when Rosina spoke Italian it shot out fast and her black eyes glittered and foamy spit puffed in the corners of her mouth. In secret, Grandpop called Rosina *a basket of goodies*. Another time he rubbed Rosina's chubby rear end with his chin. She didn't seem to mind. Acting like Grandpop had just shook her hand. This had struck Teddy as extremely interesting. The first really interesting thing since coming to Italy.

The following day he tried rubbing her rear end, too, but using his knuckles. Rosina shook a finger at him saying *bambino* like she might start to cry. It was terrible; those black eyes of hers.

One day Teddy's mother started crying and basically never stopped. She was still crying the day she told him good-bye from the living room couch, waving, and saying it was only for the summer. And how he'd have a great time living with Grandpop and Nana. It was the *living* that tipped him off. His mother didn't say visiting. It's curtains, Teddy had thought waving goodbye.

It was curtains for his father, too. His father went off to serve in Vietnam and never came back. He didn't die, just didn't come back. For a long time Teddy's mother kept their wedding picture displayed on top of the TV; eventually shoving it in a drawer. If he didn't know better, he wouldn't believe it was his mother in that picture. Back then she was thin, with shiny dark hair clipped to the side by a flower.

A fresh white hibiscus she'd tell him upon waking from one of her naps, to find her son holding the picture. In that picture his dad wore his big army hat with the wide brim. Smiling out, looking happy.

Alaska ruined us, his mother used to say. The day after that picture the Army shipped them out to Alaska. Teddy was born in the 49th state. *Cold* being pretty much all she'd tell him. And that President Eisenhower made Alaska the 49th state the exact year Teddy was born. By then she was already crying.

Rosina made clucking noises as she took away his uneaten plate of spaghetti, sliding one of fish and zucchini in front of him. I'd like to stick a zucchini inside of you, thought Teddy, keeping his eyes lowered.

Cautiously he sniffed at the food. He reached for a slice of fried bread from the basket. Nana was blabbing — something she read or saw on Italian television — who cared? He didn't. Teddy took a bite of bread crust, avoiding the fish and zucchini. Grandpop saying he better eat more or he won't be strong enough to play soccer in the fall when school starts. Nana stopped her blabbing then to give Grandpop a poke on the arm.

When Teddy finally got clear of the supper table, taking the fifty-three stone steps from the house down to the garden, running through the fig grove and along the back slope of the olive farm, toward the creek bed, the sun had gone down.

He buried Rosina's dish towel — the one she had pinned to her skirt. Snatching it from the kitchen, on his way out, while she was having a smoke in the arbor. The big silver safety pins still attached to the stained white cloth. He buried it a little ways down the creek from where he buried Bud's feather.

Without the sun beating down everything felt much cooler. The air. The air felt like something could happen. At home it was like that when summer was practically over, and school about to begin. Even though it still felt hot and summery. The fun, as everyone knew it, was done.

Teddy stood there looking toward the purple hills. And

he thought of the German kid — *Tolle*. A funny name. Like a toll booth. He kicked the ground, snorting and laughing, wondering if the German kid collected money? Then with his foot he stomped down some loose dirt around the hole of Rosina's dish towel; thinking it was weird how the creek bed didn't fill up with rain same as the villa.

The Italians have struck again he was thinking, watching some deer moving slowly along the ridge. They stopped and started, seemed to be listening. Grandpop had called them roe deer. Funny pointed antlers stuck straight up like twin antennas. Teddy wondering if they picked up radio signals? That maybe Cyrus and Billy were playing the transistor radio, lying on the bunk beds in Billy's room, and the roe deer could hear the rock and roll coming all the way from America. He stood still until they disappeared over the ridge. *Roe deer*! He was thinking that in Italy everything ran ass-backwards. Then he moved a rock to mark the spot of the grave of Rosina's dish towel.

"That's two graves," he said.

Early the next morning like it was some great expedition his grandparents set out again for the train; like two explorers on a mission, not two old fogies off to buy a couple of tomatoes and a wet bag of squid.

Teddy hung by his arms from a tree branch watching them disappear down the dirt road. I want to go home, he was thinking. Knowing there wasn't a home to go to. Not any more.

He swung his legs around the branch, hanging like a monkey, wondering how long he could stay that way. Monkeys, he knew, could hang on a long time. Forever? Suppose his grandparents didn't come back? Say they got murdered by some Italian thugs, or a band of those roving gypsies Nana always worried about. Teddy would be left an orphan. In all of Italy, only Rosina then, would he be able to point to as someone he knew.

Dropping from the tree he decided to skip breakfast. Hitching up his shorts he set off in the direction of the Tolle villa, less than a five minute walk — the next decrepit house down the line of them.

He climbed the front steps knocking on a mustard-color door. Splinters stuck out of the wood. Right away it was opened by a boy about his same age, a blond boy with skin the color of milk. And one crossed eye. So far over, the little bit of blue that showed looked stuck to the boy's nose. Teddy wondered if he could see out of it, or just out of his straight-on eye?

The good eye stayed focused on Teddy who was doing his best not to grin. Grandpop always saying how it was bad form to take pleasure in the misfortune of others. That left Teddy in a bind. He couldn't decide whether to even smile, when the German boy thrust out his chin saying, "Tolle."

"I'm Teddy."

Each boy stared at the other.

"I'm staying with my grandparents in the next villa," said Teddy. And jerked his thumb toward a clump of cypress trees he'd noticed on the way over, thinking they'd make a good bunker for playing war. Now thinking: Does this German kid have a first name? When the boy spat out: "Wilhelm."

Wilhelm. Teddy repeating it silently; swallowing it down: Wilhelm. Wilhelm.

In all his life he'd never seen such an eye as the eye of Wilhelm. For sure Grandpop would say it was a misfortune.

Just then Teddy felt a terrible itch on the side of his nose — right where Wilhelm's eye plugged in. He hesitated, needing to scratch so bad. Finally when he couldn't take it another second he scratched; fast. Gouging the side of his nose with his thumb and hoping Wilhelm didn't see.

"Don't be afraid," said Wilhelm stepping out of the house. *Stringbean* Teddy's mother used to call those kinds of boys.

Teddy thought Wilhelm sounded just like the Nazi general in that war movie THE YOUNG LIONS. He'd watched it on TV with Grandpop.

Teddy had admired the Nazi general, also the general's hat, but he couldn't understand anything because they all spoke Italian. The hat reminding Teddy of his dad's hat in the wedding picture. Then Grandpop had to go and spoil everything by telling him stuff — the Nazis and the Jews, the torture, the ovens, the gas chambers. All of it is true, Grandpop said.

Barefoot, like Teddy, the German boy was rocking back and forth on his heels, making the loose bricks of the front steps jiggle.

Teddy pointed. "That brick's about to fall out."

The German boy had on shorts, too. Except for the one crossed eye, he looked pretty much the same as Cyrus and Billy; making Teddy wonder if Grandpop had been telling the truth? When Wilhelm said, "What do you like to do?"

"I don't know."

Actually more than anything Teddy wanted to play war.

He wasn't sure it was a good idea with this German boy. As he was thinking about it, the side of his nose began itching again.

"I collect butterflies," Wilhelm was saying.

"How do you get them?"

"I catch them in my net then I press them under glass. I keep them in shadow boxes. Soon we will be unpacked of all the boxes, then I will hang them in my room."

Teddy gazed up at the second floor windows trying to decide which room belonged to Wilhelm. They all looked alike.

"How do you get the butterflies to stick on the marble?"

"Asinine." Wilhelm's straight-on eye flickered a moment. "By using a nail, of course."

And Teddy pictured the German boy sticking a nail through the body of a butterfly, forcing it to stay pinned to the marble wall.

Swinging both his arms, Wilhelm propelled off the steps in one leap. "I will need to look at the sundial first. If it is pointing toward the correct time, the butterflies will soon be swarming."

"Sundial?"

"You Americans don't have a sundial?"

Teddy shook his head.

"Come with me, I will show you."

Trotting alongside Wilhelm, who took long strides through the brambles and wild grass growing high on the grounds of the villa, they came to a stone embankment around back. Wire netting had been placed over the large, jagged stones.

"Why are those rocks covered up?" Teddy asked.

"We have to. Otherwise they will keep falling into our vegetable garden."

Teddy looked along the ground but didn't notice anything growing. "I don't see your vegetables."

The German boy began to unbutton his shirt, taking it off and draping it carefully across the wire netting. Then to Teddy's surprise, the boy removed his shorts, then his underpants, spreading them next to his shirt. In the bright sun his pale skin looked smooth and shiny as marble.

Wilhelm took hold of his penis and twirled it like an airplane propeller. "First we'll have a swim," he said.

Wow! Teddy was thinking — this German kid is nuts.

"There's no place to swim around here," he told Wilhelm. "The creek is all dried up."

"I know of a place."

"Where?"

"Not too far away, but we have to hurry if we don't want to miss the butterflies."

And pumping his arms Wilhelm started off in the direction of the hills only to break stride, ducking behind a bush. When Teddy started to follow him the boy called out: "You wait there while I defecate."

Teddy stopped short. "What do you mean?"

"Defecate. Shit. I need to shit."

"Isn't there a toilet in your house?"

Finally there was some rustling and Wilhelm stepped out from the bush. "I said don't you have a toilet in your house?"

"Of course," said Wilhelm. "Naturally we have a toilet, we're not animals. We just prefer it this way. Shit makes wonderful fertilizer."

"Huh?"

"Fertilizer. Isn't that the correct word?" Then the German boy nodded, the crossed eye digging deeper into the side of his nose; like it was trying to hide there.

"Fertilizer," Wilhelm repeated. "We shit to fertilize the garden. We give back what we get from the ground. We get very large radishes. You'll see."

I hope not! Teddy was thinking, deciding not to mention a word of it to Grandpop who could get really uptight. If someone happened to get the runs, Grandpop went straight for the bottle of lye to scrub out the toilet. If he heard about this fertilizer shit business he might make Teddy stay away from the German boy. Then he'd have no one again.

"To the sundial!" Wilhelm shouted swinging his arm high like a flag.

"What about a butterfly net?" Teddy ran around in front of him to get another look at the eye. Even more hidden; exciting him a great deal. "Where's your butterfly net, Wilhelm?"

"You will know very soon for yourself," he said pushing on through the grass.

Teddy scrambled after him. "Do I get to try and catch some?"

"That depends."

"On what? On what does it depend, Wilhelm?"

The boy tipped his head toward the sky. "Whether or not we become comrades."

Comrades! Teddy felt a fresh burst of excitement. This was far better than playing dirt-bombs with Cyrus and Billy. This Wilhelm kid could easily be a Nazi. It both thrilled and terrified him.

"I'm no Jew," said Teddy. "Just so's you know that."

"Jews don't bother me." Then Wilhelm stopped walking to announce: "The sundial."

Sticking up through the high grass Teddy could make out a strange looking object. As they got closer he saw it was made of greenish metal. The German boy leaned over it.

"See the way it casts its shadow to tell the time."

Wondering which eye he was using, Teddy asked, "Couldn't you just wear a watch?"

"This way is better. This is the way the ancients told time." Wilhelm continued to stare down.

Bugs had begun swarming. Teddy swatted at his arms. He was getting fidgety. He wanted to bag butterflies not stand around in the weeds looking at a dumb sundial. He was sorry now that he skipped breakfast. He felt hot and sweaty and hungry all at the same time.

"Where's this swimming place? What is it, a lake or something?"

Wilhelm straightened up. "Everything is in order. We can swim and still see the butterflies."

"It's a lake, right?"

He had to trot to keep up with Wilhelm. He was thinking about the only lake he'd ever been to — Lake Ronkonkoma. Going with Cyrus and Billy, driven by Cyrus' father in their station wagon. A lake his mother claimed was polluted. Polluted long before Teddy was ever born. Kids get polio from lakes, she had told him, and that he'd be swimming at his own risk.

"Is it a clean lake you're taking me to, Wilhelm?"

"Not a lake."

Soon they came to a clearing. Teddy saw what looked like a swimming pool in the middle of all the grass. At least what was left of a swimming pool. A dried out rubber hose trickled brownish water into the cavernous, cracked cement hole.

Teddy stepped closer. The water in the pool looking impossibly low; even for wading; forget swimming. But Wilhelm was already making tracks down the steps leading into the pool. He stood at the bottom and grinned, the dirty-looking water reaching

61

only as far as his thighs. "Delightful," he said slapping the water.

Teddy scratched where a bug had bitten his elbow. Bright colored tiles with pictures covered the sides of the pool and part way down. "What's with those tiles?"

"They tell the story of the Roman Empire."

"No kidding." Teddy bent to have a closer look. He knew a little bit about the Roman Empire. The Christians and the lions, and Julius Caesar. Some of the pool tiles had warriors holding shields. He reached out to touch an especially colorful tile. "This must be the gladiators."

"Correct!"

Grinning, Teddy stretched out on his belly in the grass reaching toward another one. A tree tile. It felt bumpy. "Nah! I wanna see a chariot race, I wanna see those chariots in action."

"It's all here." And Wilhelm spread his arms like a king surveying his kingdom.

Teddy strained forward on his belly toward another interesting tile, one of soldiers marching.

"You should come in," said Wilhelm. "The water is wonderful."

Polio water, thought Teddy. "No thanks." Besides he was busy scouting gladiators. "What's that one?"

Bracing his hands against the tiles he shimmied further down, anxious to touch an especially interesting one he felt sure was Julius Caesar, when a sudden explosive sound shattered the air. His hands flew out and Teddy tumbled into the pool.

What he remembered next was Bud flying past with all his yellow feathers spiked and smoking.

When he opened his eyes he saw Wilhelm. Wilhelm leaning close to his face. The one crossed eye gone missing; the way his dad had gone missing. Then Teddy realized he was wet; feeling the crackling dry grass underneath him.

"You fell into the swimming pool when I farted," Wilhelm said. "I carried you out. I thought you were dead."

Teddy stared into the missing eye. Veins crawling through the white part were like stalks of grass. He thought of the Jews then, crawling along the ground, dying in the packed trains while begging for mercy. He wondered if the trains were running today? Or had the Italians struck again?

"If I was a Jew would you still carry me out of the pool?"

"Why of course," said Wilhelm, unblinking. §

Within You
Without You

A long time ago she had been part of an entourage that traveled to India with the Beatles. She had been invited. It's not exactly a known fact. There were other people who tagged along and received terrific publicity, had their photo in LOOK or LIFE, wrote articles, books, gave interviews that generally exploited the Beatles, the Mahareeshi and India; for what that was worth. Some forty years later, Mrs. Calcutta almost can't believe it herself — she was there. Another little known fact: there were two Mahareeshis on the scene. The second Mahareeshi (dubbed *the lesser Mahareeshi* by Beatle George) had given her her new name: *Mrs. Calcutta*; telling her: *You are our mother and our father.* She had traveled to India as Katie Rose Klugen, and she left transformed. Epic.

When you've been on the inside track of something that big, that momentous — historic, really; well there's never again the need to worry about catching the last errant train. India. And she had literally imploded, all blocks to her mystic pathways released. Up till that point her life had been fairly humdrum.

Last year Mrs. Calcutta returned to this Queens neighborhood where she'd grown up. Her elderly mother had fallen ill eventually passing from complications of pneumonia. The two bedroom co-op left in the will. There were no siblings. Crumbly with age, the roomy old place had a nice park view from a triple window in the living room and was still furnished mostly with her mother's things. Some of them, like the red lacquer Chinese coffee table, pretty damned nice.

She ran her hand across the smooth-as-glass finish, remembering the story about her dad shipping it home to her mother, during the Second World War. She saw him in China haggling over the red table in a marketplace where chickens hung by string fastened to their ankles. She wondered a moment if chickens were plentiful during that period? Her dad had been in Army *supply* and knew how to get things. After the war, he'd somehow procured this apartment; though decent housing in and around New York City had been scarce. Then he left for good when she was about three or four.

Well, Mrs. Calcutta had options. She could stay on in Queens or sell the place. The town itself was becoming problematic. Filthy. An almost deliberate attempt to ruin what had been a green and grassy oasis just beyond city limits. Accumulating trash on sidewalks and along the curbs, graffiti showing up everywhere depressed her. Most buildings had those steel window guards that clamped down at night to keep out junkies.

In the mystical trade for many years, she had recently rented a small storefront on one of the main drags. Minus a window guard, already hers had been smashed. So much for the honor system, she'd thought, phoning for replacement glass and a guard to be installed. Not that she had anything in particular against junkies. These days, more than ever, she understood the great societal need for drugs; though it was probably half a lifetime since Mrs. Calcutta let even a mere joint rest between her lips. *Been there, done that* was her stock reply.

Back then. When she was this petite waif-girl, skinny and flat chested with all those protruding bones. Elbows, knees, chin, cheekbones. Raffish hair chopped off in a pixie-cut, huge saucer eyes lined with kohl; eyes that took up a good deal of the surface area on her face. Somewhat coincidentally (though Mrs. Calcutta believed in no such phenomenon) around that same time a certain artist was becoming rich and famous painting faces with impossibly large round eyes, that found their way onto greeting cards.

So the summer after high school graduation, she'd hopped

a plane to LA, ended up in Malibu, at this hip party where the Beatles happened to be partying. Her face striking a chord with John Lennon. He'd sniffed her hair like no tomorrow, wanted to know was she *the face* for the waif-faced model? Eventually George got into the act, too, but later. Each in his own way and his own time. Even the flowing Mahareeshi in his robe was bewitched, inviting her to come along to India. *Sacred.* He'd murmured it into her third eye.

On a train that may have been traveling from Mirat to Ranpur, or Mayapore to Pankot, the Mahareeshi plucked another Mahareeshi practically out of thin air. That second Mahareeshi seemed to float, materializing from out of the miniscule cloak room in the stuffy train compartment. Naturally, being the Beatles, they had taken over all the first class walnut-paneled railroad cars. Everything very *British colonial,* leftover from the days... velvet train seats worn down to shiny, mirrors' darkly mottled glass, bronze wall sconces and other accoutrements decayed and moldering. Centuries of dust in the folds of the train curtains. Not that anyone on that spiritual junket seemed to notice, or care. Dirt! Dust! It had no significance.

By way of explanation, regarding the second Mahareeshi, George told her *the lesser Maharesshi* was a true Maharesshi all the same.

Ringo, juggling drum sticks in the bong-filled air, said *fucking A* more than once, as if to confirm the second Mahareeshi's good standing.

Paul sat alone and silent. Brooding in his seat. Or perhaps just sleepy.

John, in her memory, inexplicably missing from that moment.

At any rate, the lesser Mahareeshi, chubby in the way of the upper Mahareeshi, kept smiling and smiling. He picked out Mrs. Calcutta to smile at from almost the first instant. He bobbed up and down like a buoy.

There are other girls on this train, why don't you smile at Marianne Faithfull? had crossed her mind.

Yet for all his intense cheer there was trouble brewing in his inkpot eyes. He often looked cloudy and unsteady, mumbling in his native tongue, and sometimes he called her *Mister Calcutta;* once requesting she wear a necktie to bed.

At that, all the Beatles except Paul had burst out laughing. Then Paul said *How bloody original* and told the lesser Mahareeshi to *Give it a rest.* Then John told Paul: *You're confusing things.* The lesser Mahareeshi continued to be confused throughout most of the journey. India. All very strange and wonderful.

Of course after a time things began winding down, as things will do. Disagreements arose. Where to chant, the hill or the garden? Which foods to eat, who not to invite to dinner.

As for Mrs. Calcutta, some private arrangement had been worked out by John and George, though of the two, George came to her less frequently, engrossed as he was in what would become "Within You Without You." She'd heard those particular words spoken but didn't know beyond them at the time.

And, what of it? She liked guessing. Would it be John or George parting the mosquito netting that draped her bed? Uncertainty making it all the more wondrous! Two Beatles at her beck and call! Or, she at two Beatle's beck and call! Either way, it was practically a spontaneous miracle (though Mrs. Calcutta did not believe in miracles). Devising her own secret game, she placed roots in her ears to blot out their voices, keeping her eyes shut. Revelation coming only with the kiss.

Then one night after a solid week of mud weather, the lesser Mahareeshi beat it out of the compound. Who could blame him? He'd been taking heaps of abuse from the upper Mahareeshi who fingered him for this or that infraction. As minor as leaving the cap off the toothpaste! His absence not discovered until morning.

By then things had pretty much cooled across the board, the news services picking up and reporting trouble from within the enlightened circle. Someone (disgruntled servant?) leaked information. Someone banged a hole in Ringo's snare drum.

In her opinion he handled the situation well. *No big deal* was all he said. Quietly, meditative sounding. Though under that cool friendly exterior Ringo's nerve endings never stopped jumping. Mrs. Calcutta saw them doing a sort of jitterbug movement. And sometimes they acted like ball bearings that kept trying but missing their connective point.

At last, the inevitable goodbyes. She scarcely felt hers, though her mouth had opened appropriately, the right words poured out, her arms had extended to give and receive hugs. Then Mrs. Calcutta flew away to Hong Kong. She'd always wanted to see the Chinese junk boats sliding through the harbor in a purple sunset. She had money in her purse (a quite considerable sum) thanks to John and George. After a couple of weeks in a noisy flat in Kowloon, where the neighbors strung washing across the balconies, she packed for Macao. She'd heard Macao called *practically prehistoric* and that sounded good; Kowloon under siege from street construction day and night. One thing she'd learned from India: she required the quiet breath.

Built low to the ground, and dusty, Macao had the look and feel of a Mexican border town. What motivated Mrs. Calcutta to stay on a few years, she still can't explain; but stay she did, operating a small truck stop café for people coming off the tour buses in need of light refreshment (after Macao she would put down stakes in seven major cities then broadly called *The Orient)*. Why that particular region of the world had called to her, she couldn't say.

And, in all honesty, she couldn't say she missed a one of them. Not John, brilliant and ethereal. Or sweetly sensitive George. Or the other two Beatles who'd become lumped together like sticky oatmeal. Elusive reasoning. In fact, Mrs. Calcutta did not like saying the names of the other two out loud. She also didn't miss either Mahareeshi. Her time spent in India was her own to claim. Grown used to her new name, and deciding to keep it, while in Macao, she began noticing things differently.

It started with the people stepping down from the tour buses. Many looked frustrated, unhappy, the elderly in particular who struggled with the somewhat steep bus steps, as if it meant life or death. And she would look and immediately know everything. Infancy down to their last rattling breath. Spread out nice and orderly in front of her.

Besides the orange swizzle drinks, Chinese beer, and paper thin sandwiches, she had something else to offer people. Tacking a sign on the flimsy, termite infested veranda post: MYSTICAL READINGS (free).

"I'm not sure about that," said Mrs. Calcutta.

At her storefront location in Queens, sitting opposite a heavy-set, middle-aged male client, the table draped in batik-cloth, she was feeling squeezed. The single room had required a separation so she'd hired a carpenter to partition off the waiting space from the consult space. It turned out all wrong. The waiting area now way too large, the consult area too tiny to comfortably accommodate both of them, a table, a pair of folding chairs. Not to mention the man's overt misery adding to the tight feeling.

For a moment her mind shifted to India. Its open fields, wild and expansive, as seen from the train windows long ago. She tried adjusting her chair but it was already smack against the partition wall, the fake wood paneling with its flat bulbous knots like lips sucking air out of the space. She took some quick breaths in and out.

She had once known the Beatles. People passed it along to other people, it brought people in for a reading. As the story went, she had found her spiritual awakening in India on that pilgrimage. What the heck! It wasn't quite like that.

The upper Mahareeshi, quickly growing bored with her, had wanted to toss her off the train. Literally. Every time he came within ten feet, she was forced to change cars. It was exhausting. He kept calling her *idiot* over virtually nothing. Then he called her *stupid idiot*, all on account of a small fire (easily put out) after she accidentally dropped a match in the lavatory bin. Everyone standing by benignly while she sobbed. Even John and George, the train rocking, the Mahareeshi tearing into her. Soon, maybe a day or so after, the appearance of the *lesser Mahareeshi*. Nobody thought much of it. Not then, not now.

The news services covering the pilgrimage had printed a most unflattering photo of her, half-kneeling in the fields beside a young spotted deer, her head tipped at an incongruous angle. The headline reading *Beatle Girl and Billy Goat, Is it Love?* Goat?

The implication was hideous. The Beatles had found it funny. The article went on to label her a *typical American malcontent*, mentioning the lavatory fire and hinting that she might be a pyromaniac with tendencies toward bestiality (she'd only wanted to hug the little deer). In those days bad publicity did not magically convert to good publicity and cash. When she thought of the deer now, she thought the timing unlucky.

Best to keep everything big secretive; that's how to get through this life, she thought. She was trying hard to smile at the unhappy man across the table. *Know the unknown and taste the unwelcome* — it had stayed with her all these years, a teaching from one of the Mahareeshis. Most likely the upper Mahareeshi.

"Please, you have to tell me." Across from her the man looked flushed and sweaty, his bottom lip quivering.

Mrs. Calcutta shut her eyes to get away from him. What could she say? She couldn't see his wife, Jodi Lynn. The wife wasn't coming across. A woman he called a princess, and saying she was unfaithful to him. He was certain. But he came to Mrs. Calcutta to be one hundred percent sure. Children are at stake, he told her.

She shook her head and opened her eyes. "Sorry, I'm still

not getting it. I'll give you back your money."

"My money?" He seemed about to break down. If he fell against the partition wall, chances were pretty good he'd break that, too. And if he took back his money, it would negate other things, important things, that she'd already confirmed. Reducing the whole reading to a big fat zero. Failure. She wondered if his princess, Jodi Lynn, ever called him *fat*?

Then probably the first time in forty years, Mrs. Calcutta thought of "Within You Without You." George's words infiltrating the tight space. What he called that space between us, all his dreamy wall of illusion stuff.

She licked her dry lips. If the man took his money back, he would leave with less than he came with. He knew as much, too. That she could see quite clearly. Why the hell couldn't she see the rest of his life?

With some difficulty he stood up partially dragging the batik tablecloth along with him. Embarrassed, he tried smoothing it; then ran a hand across his balding pate. "You keep the money," he told Mrs. Calcutta. "I'm going home now, to start to trust my wife."

Maybe it was his hand moving the sparse hairs on his head that caused her insides to shiver. Again she thought of India, its hills and soft blowing grasses. Then John, George and the others crowded in, chanting, chanting, everyone as one. Before the whole thing came loose.

She saw flames latch onto white bed sheets and heard a woman's shrill laughter ring out. "Does Jodi Lynn have a lot of red hair?"

His adams apple jumped, a kind of delirium in his throat.

"Long and red, real red, not dyed or anything." The man stood straighter. "You can see her now? It isn't good, is it?"

"It isn't good. But it's not forever," said Mrs. Calcutta standing, too. §

Slow Burn

Anne's two beagle hounds are driving everyone insane with their yowling to get outside in the snow. Treading lightly, as usual, with my sister, I hear Mother tell her: "Put the blessed beasts in the garage."

At the rear of the property, the garage is connected to the house by a long driveway that meanders under a wide cement portico, past stone walls thick with creeping vines. If it weren't for the two, giant blue spruce trees smoldering out front, the place would be the perfect winter setting.

Since yesterday the trees have been doing their slow burn. A freakish winter lightning storm sparked the phone wires, igniting some leaning branches. Dad called the fire department twice. Twice they came out in full regalia: trucks, hats, sirens, hoses, the works. Yet wisps of smoke continue to spiral out of the trees. I don't get it.

Most of what goes on around here, I don't get. I'm just back for a visit — on account of my cast. Thick plaster encasing one leg from the top of my thigh down to my toes. All because of three little stitches.

"Three little pigs," I say, trying to wiggle my toes inside

the cast. Three little stitches near my inside ankle bone; to repair a deep tear from another freakish accident involving Jack; and the bathroom in my apartment in Philadelphia.

When the stitches finally healed and I still couldn't walk without agonizing pain shooting up my leg, there was a new diagnosis: severed nerve damage. With lots of depressing talk about casts, half-casts, walking-casts, braces, limps. The doctor said I should expect to end up walking with a limp. Not too good for an aspiring actress, I'd told him; imagining myself on stage playing invalid roles the rest of my life. But now that I've been getting around on crutches, and getting down the stairs by sliding on my butt, a limp doesn't sound half bad.

"You could make it look very sexy," Anne told me. She's a still-life painter who sees sex everywhere. Her bowls of fruit ooze like intimate body parts.

What *has* been bad, is this *sabbatical* at my childhood home; my overly concerned parents; a sister, who, at thirty-three still lives here, controlling things with her simpering smile and iron will. The first five minutes back in my old room she had to know everything.

"Tell me about Jack," she said, smoothing her long, extra-blonde hair and making herself comfortable in the window seat.

I leaned my crutches against the knotty-pine footboard and fell backward onto the mattress. "There's nothing to tell."

Anne just smiled nestling deeper into the toss pillows. Looking coy she picked up my old brown teddy bear *Mister Wickets*. It was to *Mister Wickets* that she directed her interrogation.

"Mister Wickets, she said on the phone that Jack dislodged a soap dish from the wall."

"Anne, chill!"

"Well, how did that soap dish end up inside her ankle?"

Using my good leg I kicked at the crutches knocking them to the floor.

"Mister Wickets, she's getting angry with us. All we want to know are the particulars. It isn't every day someone is left crippled after just three stitches."

Tired and stressed from the bumpy ride on the commuter jet, where every jolt of turbulence cemented my fear of not making it to Long Island — not alive, anyway — there on top of my old blue quilt I let out a moan. I hadn't planned to. But once it was out in the open, hanging in the air between me and my sister, I accepted it for what it was: a true animal moan. The kind I used to make with Jack while he plied my body with tenderness. Remembering how good that felt, I whimpered — another animal sound — but more like what might come out of Mister Wickets, if he could make noises.

I guess Anne felt sorry for me then because she let up, sitting Mister Wickets back on the dresser. Though she did cross his one leg over the other, in a rather jaunty pose; leaving me alone with my misery. All that happened a few days ago, before the trees began to burn.

***

I wake up feeling like I haven't slept, struggling out of bed, crutching into my bathroom to get the water glass and a fifth of JOHNNIE WALKER I stashed in the tub. Pouring scotch two-thirds up the glass, holding it tightly, I crutch toward the front window — the window seat where Anne did her shtick. Propped up on the crutches I'm sipping and watching smoke spiral out of the tops of the spruce trees.

Thin wispy smoke. Charcoal-colored against a colorless sky — like smoke from two tepees in the snow. At any moment an Indian princess and her warrior might emerge with their fat little black-haired papoose. What does emerge, from around the trees, is a family of deer — at least I take them for a family; two are large and loping, a smaller one has to hop to keep up. My eyes moisten, and I take a swig of scotch and think about Jack and the kids we might have had together.

"Lee!" calls Mother from downstairs, "come join us for a nice breakfast!" Mother likes things orderly: three square meals, clean sheets on Saturday, daily teeth flossing; that sort of thing. When I don't answer right away, I can hear her climbing the stairs to come get me.

"I'm all right!" I shove the glass of scotch behind Mister Wickets on the dresser. Sorry for the irritation in my voice.

She means well. It's just that I don't want breakfast. The smoky taste of scotch is all I want right now, it seems to fit with the smoldering trees.

She pokes her head in, a frown wrinkling her forehead, her little half-glasses slipping down her chip of a nose as she takes in my unwashed, still-not-dressed appearance.

Smiling quickly to cover, she says, "Quiche and a glass of fresh-squeezed orange juice will put the roses back in your cheeks."

"I'll be down in a minute."

"Can I help you put on a robe, dear?"

Gritting my teeth I shake my head. Nothing can help me. I lean heavily on the crutches, my arm pits rubbed raw. Before the accident Jack used to kiss them and I'd laugh hysterically because it tickled so much, telling him: *Don't! You'll get poisoned from my deodorant!*

"Can I help you downstairs?" Mother is looking doubtful about my ability to make it alone. And I'm thinking that I don't remember any elevators in the house, so how the hell have I been doing it this past week? I give her one of my own looks and she retreats in silence. Then grabbing the glass of scotch from behind Mister Wickets, I drain it dry.

At least the stairs aren't carpeted — carpets making butt sliding a lot more difficult. My apartment building in Philly has this tight-weave carpet down the halls and stairs, making rug burns through my sweat pants. By that time Jack was officially out — *care-giver* not in his job description. He never got to see my butt in that compromised condition.

Already in the dining room, Dad and Anne are seated at the oval Chippendale table. Why Mother insists on having every meal in the dining room... even breakfast...

Dad grins and salutes me. "Lee-Lee, good to have you up and about." From malaria he caught in Korea during *that war,* Dad's totally bald — a little round smiling Buddha.

Under the dining room archway I grin back at him weakly, squeezing the knot in the belt of my chenille robe and hoping no one can smell scotch on my breath. "Thanks, Dad." I know he's waiting to hear this. "It's good to be up and about."

"That's the girl, that's the spirit!"

Oh, no. I can feel myself starting to deflate under the weight of his pep. Dad's older than most grandfathers. Amazingly, he's still a weekend sailor. Even during winter, with his sloop safely in dry-dock, you always get the feeling he'll find some way of hoisting the mainsail, tacking her out through the channel, out to sea. *The Ruby* she's called. Kind of a double entendre — after Mother whose name is Ruby; and the fact that he always refers to her as *my gem.*

Sitting with her arms folded Anne's looking all dolled-up in a red cashmere twin-set; her extra-blonde hair braided in one flat plait.

"I'd like to get this meal over with," she says. "That's if Lee ever decides to sit down."

Murmuring, "Sorry," I crutch over to the table where my chair has been conveniently pulled out in advance.

At first this totally annoyed me — this taking away of my independence. Now I've gotten used to it. I no longer give a shit. Shoving the crutches under the table, pretending to have an appetite, I say, "Those quiches look great!"

Mother beams and takes her place across from me at the table. "There's spinach and Lorraine, fresh out of the oven."

"Which has the onions?" I ask.

"Lorraine," says Anne, cutting a large wedge of that very quiche and sliding it onto her plate. "You still have problems with onions giving you heartburn?"

Clearing my throat I decide to ignore that, taking my time removing the napkin ring, arranging the pinkish linen napkin carefully in my lap. "These are beautiful napkins, Mother. Did you get them on your last trip to Ireland?"

"No, dear, they were part of my wedding trousseau. My own mother put them into my Hope Chest. Can you imagine! Young girls used to have Hope Chests! So long ago." She's fingering the double-edge of her napkin lovingly, like it has an actual soul; then saying with palpable sadness, "There used to be twelve. I think a few got lost in the wash."

"Hah!" says Dad. "My socks disappear in the wash, too."

Mother sighs, placing the napkin next to her plate. "Oh, Hank, well. That's enough of that."

"Why are the trees still burning?" I ask.

"And that's enough of that," Mother says.

Now this has got me totally intrigued. Planting my elbows on the table I lean forward. "I don't understand. Why can't we talk about the trees?"

With her mouth full of quiche, Anne says, "We'll talk about those trees after *you* tell us what happened with Jack." She chews and swallows, her eyes turning dreamy.

And I get this uneasy jiggly sort of heat sensation inside my chest. I'm wondering if all the scotch drinking has finally started to burn up vital organs, when Anne says, "By the way, Lee, if you're finished with Jack I wouldn't mind a shot."

Looking around the table I'm thinking: Have you all cracked up? "I'm not hungry," I say.

"Now, now," says Mother.

"Now now what?" My voice has grown louder. "What's that mean *now now*? Sounds like some language from somewhere like the Fiji Islands." Reaching under the table for the crutches, I struggle to get on my feet.

With his head tilted back Dad is saying, "Fiji Islands, Fiji Islands." Like it's meaningful or something.

"I'm not playing this stupid game of yours," I tell them. "Whatever it is. I'm going back to Philadelphia where trees aren't left to burn."

Benjamin Franklin, his face framed in a cameo, flashes through my mind. Benjamin Franklin — plastered all over the city of Philadelphia. Resting on the crutches I tell them, "Benjamin Franklin would never sit here stuffing quiche in his face while two beautiful trees are left to burn."

Mother gets this stricken look. She pops out of her chair and comes to stand beside me. "It's not a game, dear." She brushes some strands of hair away from my face. "It's just best not to hold onto things. This holding onto things, it can cause cancer."

"Cancer?"

Dad pipes up, then. "Take your sister, here. Breast cancer at her age."

"Anne has breast cancer?" I feel like the top of my head is about to come off.

"Yes, but it's not going to stop me," my sister says. "I'm taking my chemo and if the time comes I'll take my radiation."

Erect at the table she's looking perfectly confident; like she's just explained a new painting technique.

"Now what about Jack and your accident?" says Anne.

Pushing on the crutches I brace my back against the mahogany sideboard. Swallowing hard I say, "It was nothing. Nothing. Jack loosened the soap dish while he was taking a bath and it fell out while I was taking a shower."

I can see Anne pondering this as she scoops melon balls onto her plate. I'm wondering how she can eat so much while taking chemo. Isn't chemo supposed to make you so nauseous you'd rather die? Anne is eating like she's starving.

She looks up from the melon balls. "Exactly how did Jack loosen the soap dish?"

"He pulled himself up on that bar that's a part of it."

"The grab-bar," says Dad.

"Yeah," I say. "Except it's not meant for grabbing. It's

really just a place to hang your wash cloth. Period."

I didn't want to go into all that. Now that I have, I'm feeling more miserable. I gaze down at my cast. At my bloated-looking foot; big and ugly in the white gym sock. One of Jack's socks. Mine too small to fit over the plaster.

"Jack's an intelligent man," Mother says. "He directs plays. He should've known better."

Jack's a selfish bastard I'm thinking; picturing him soaking for hours in my tub, his long spidery legs, pointed knees poking through the water. Soaking. Till it turned cold and gray and scummy. He would add more hot. More and more. I kept meaning to call *the Super* to have that soap dish re-cemented. I really kept meaning to.

"You haven't had your quiche," Mother tells me.

"I don't want any."

While standing under a spray of warm water, the bright winter sunlight coming in through the bathroom window, the soap dish came crashing out of the wall. One in — one out. Sharp, with its edge of hardened cement, it sliced the skin on the vulnerable inner part of my ankle. Cutting deep, deep into a nerve. Blood gushing, splattering the white bathroom, the tub filled with it, blood everywhere. My blood. Out there. At last. For Jack to see.

The beginning of the end.

Turning my head slowly, I look at my family gathered together in this room too full of polished mahogany. "I should have called *the Super* the minute Jack loosened the soap dish."

And I'm remembering a book I saw before the accident, in the window of a bookstore around the corner from my apartment. The title had caught my eye: *Accidentally on Purpose*. I didn't buy the book though it intrigued me. I was in a hurry that day. Before the accident I was always in a hurry.

"Accidentally on purpose," I mutter softly.

Could it be, that somewhere, in the deepest part of my heart, I'd wished all along for Jack to leave me?

As I'm mulling this over the beagles come bounding into the dining room. Anne bends to pet both dog heads at the same time. I look at her two breasts, small and safe behind red cashmere; then shivering, I look away.

"I'm really sorry to hear about your cancer," I say.

"I'm not worried." She looks like she actually means this; it gives me chills.

"Well I'm worried about *my* life," I say. Suddenly wanting

to talk and talk. "And I'm worried about the trees."

Dad grunts and pushes his chair back and stands up. "Stop worrying about those damned trees. I don't want to hear another word about them. They'll burn until they've had enough. And that will be that." §

Elvis Out Of The Meditation Garden

"There's got to be a way to get my teeth whiter," Elvis is saying, running a finger across his top row. "I'm *The King*. All those young punks have whiter teeth now than I do. Do somethin'."

I look over at my boyfriend Ramey, who says, "He's right, you know. He is *The King* — we have to do something. We stole him. He's our responsibility."

Ensconced on his throne backstage at the Elm Street Community Theatre — a throne banged out of scrap lumber leftover from a prior show and spray-painted a shiny gold by Ramey — *The King* is looking less than pleased. He's been out of the MEDITATION GARDEN a total of three days and four nights — (think of this as a motel stay Ramey told him).

Elvis staying most of the time on his throne tucked between the racks of costumes, while Ramey and I are doing our darndest to keep Elvis happy. Me in the skimpy outfits. Both of us bringing in all his favorite foods. The backstage area set to look as much like GRACELAND as possible — several wooden trees, from our PETER PAN production, have been placed in Elvis's line of vision; as well as a stuffed wire deer from our Christmas pageant, and a scrim from the opening scene of SHOWBOAT. Ramey at first disparaging the scrim, repeating: No way. No way would a river boat come into play at GRACELAND. I had to convince him. The big white Showboat, I said, with those white posts along the rail, it's highly reminiscent of those big white columns that grace GRACELAND. Elvis will relate, I assured him.

"So what do you hear of Priscilla?" His head cocked to the side, he's flashing that famous grin.

Jeez, I'm thinking; my heart palpitating from all the Elvis energy sparking the dingy backstage. In his skin-tight, white satin jumpsuit with the fringe he's bare to the waist. "Priscilla? Why I believe she's doing just fine."

Before we brought Elvis back, we made a pact — do not tell anything that could be construed by Elvis as even mildly upsetting. We wanted Elvis to enjoy his stay; for however long that might be. We also made another pact. If necessary, we were in this for the long haul. Ramey adding: It's kind of like taking the vows, for better or worse... I knew what was going through *his* mind. Not yet, I had told him, turning away in bed.

"Give me that mirror again, will you darlin'," says Elvis.

"Sure, Elvis." I run to get a swivel mirror from the dressing room.

When I return Ramey is standing behind him, massaging one of Elvis's shoulder rotator cuffs. It got banged a little when we lifted him out of the ground.

"That feels real good," Elvis is saying. "You know, in the early days, Colonel Tom Parker used to massage me every night on the road." He winks.

Ramey raises an eyebrow.

"I saw that!" Shrieking with laughter Elvis flips his white cape over the back of his throne.

"What do you mean, Elvis?" Ramey's playing dumb.

"I saw that eyebrow go *pop*, boy."

"But, Elvis, I was standing behind you."

"That's the neat trick about comin' back. I can do all kindsa stuff I couldn't do before."

"No kidding, Elvis?" Hoping to appeal to his kingly nature I kneel before him as a supplicant. "Do you want to share?"

"You darlin'."

Elvis grabs my breast quite matter-of-factly. Because he's used to getting anything he wants, I take this as the supreme compliment. It must mean Elvis wants me. I must be at least as desirable as the long list of babes in Elvis's love arena. "Wow, Elvis," I say.

Looking stern, Ramey clears his throat. "King, it's time for your lunch." Trying to divert Elvis's attention away from my breasts and onto the thick shakes and burgers and fries he missed so much while being away.

"Priscilla had a nice pair, too," Elvis is saying, screwing up his face in some old memory.

"Go on, Maura, go get Elvis his food." Ramey jerking a thumb toward the lit EXIT sign between flats.

"I'm sorry, Elvis," I say softly. Smiling, I gently disengage his hand.

I am sorry. Elvis had a nice way of holding onto my body. Not rough, or demanding. Just natural. Like you'd hold a door-knob on a door you meant to go through.

"Extra cheese!" shouts Elvis forgetting me right away.

That's the thing. He's back with all these supernatural powers — like seeing what you're doing clear on the other side of the wings. Then he can't remember where he put his comb. It's eerie, I told Ramey the other night, it's like he's possessed of certain powers and dispossessed of common knowledge. Ramey answering: It's all that boozing and doping from the old days, plus the constant TV watching that killed off too many brain cells. In Ramey's opinion.

I'm not so sure. I think there's more to Elvis than meets the eye; though I'm not inclined to say; not till I have more proof. That Elvis has kept his incredible sexual prowess alive, there's no denying.

"Onions?" I ask him, swinging my purse onto my shoulder.

"The works, darlin'!" Elvis winking at me.

I leave through the stage door, climbing the cement steps up to the parking lot. Accumulated wet leaves make the steps treacherous. Next to a Chinese restaurant that borders the parking lot there's a cycle shop. I picture Elvis astride one of the big black

Harleys and get all tingly in my crotch. We tried some General Tso's chicken on Elvis's first day back. It gave him heartburn. Ramey believes we should stick to basics — what Elvis was used to eating; at least for the time being. He wants *The King* in tip-top shape for his big performance.

I get Elvis his food and bring it back to the theatre. A light mist has dampened my hair. I hand Elvis the McDONALD'S bag because he gets a big kick out of unwrapping each food item himself, like a kid unwrapping his Christmas presents. I smile, smoothing the frizz in my ponytail.

"Priscilla had bootiful dark hair." He says this with a mouth full of burger.

Standing next to the throne, Ramey's body sort of jack-knifes. "Did you say *bootiful*, Elvis?"

Elvis nods, chewing happily.

"That's because he had a mouthful," I add quickly.

Elvis swallows, grinning at both of us.

"Say it again, Elvis," Ramey tells him. "Say what you said about Priscilla's hair. That it's *boo...*" Ramey is gesturing, coaxing it out of him. "C'mon, Elvis, say it... *boo...*"

"Bootiful."

"Whoa!" Ramey shoots me a look.

"He's just putting us on," I say, "isn't that right, Elvis?"

Nodding agreeably, Elvis rips the top off the fries container, chucking it over his shoulder. Eating the fries so fast I don't think he's bothering to chew.

"There could be a problem," Ramey is saying. "There's song lyrics to consider. People might expect certain lapses, on account of his personal history and all. But they'll want HEART-BREAK HOTEL to sound..."

"Hotbweak Hotel," Elvis chimes in.

"Fuck!" says Ramey.

"That's not necessary," I say, bending to pick up the empty fries container Elvis has chucked along with the lid. "You're going to upset him. Then what?"

Ramey takes a swing at the wire deer. It sways but doesn't fall down. "We made an investment in him," he says rubbing his scraped knuckles.

"I'm *The King*." And Elvis gets up from his throne, stretching, picking food out of his teeth.

Knowing that Elvis would need certain things Ramey

bought an acoustical guitar from a re-sale shop. Getting it now, I walk toward Elvis offering the guitar.

"Look, Elvis, look what we bought you."

Elvis stares it down like I'm offering him an orangutan. He clicks the heels of his white go-go boots, stepping back, putting up his hands as if shielding himself from danger. "No, no! Not that."

"I don't believe this," says Ramey.

Pressing forward with the guitar I say, "We wanted to get you an electric one, Elvis, but they ran a little too high for our budget." I apologize some more. Then I step closer, noticing Elvis's face has turned an unnatural shade.

"You look a little pale," I tell him.

"He looks like a ghost," Ramey mutters. "What a disaster."

"Make-up covers a multitude of sins," I say.

"I have sinned before God and man." And Elvis staggers, and we both rush to grab his arms, pushing him back on his throne where he slumps with his head dropped forward. Very un-Elvislike. If he were an actor in our troupe, and I was directing the scene, I would have to say he looks dejected.

"Poor Elvis." I kneel in front of the throne. Hoping he won't be able to resist me, that he'll take hold of my breast again. Being Elvis-ish again. The Elvis we all knew. The Elvis *before* lunch.

"It was premature to give him that guitar," Ramey is saying. "He needs more time to adjust. It's been what — how long?"

"I been dead twenty eight years," Elvis says.

"You ain't dead now," says Ramey.

"Who says?" A smile flickers across Elvis's lips. Not his usual flashy wild grin but a shadowy secretive smile.

"I am dead in the eyes of God and man," says Elvis.

"Well, we're man. And we can see you. Well, not Maura, that is, she's a woman."

"So glad you noticed." I glower up at Ramey, picking at the guitar on the floor beside me. I have failed to entice Elvis — he just looks tired on his throne. Maybe the sounds of the guitar will reopen some buried instinct. I pick at a few more strings.

But Elvis has shut his eyes. In a moment he's snoring loudly.

"Well that worked. You put him right to sleep."

"You put me to sleep every time we go to bed," I say evenly.

Frowning, Ramey pulls himself up tall. "What are we gonna do about him? Something's wrong. For sure he'll flub the lyrics."

I sigh, shrugging; watching Elvis sleep. He looks sweet with his head lolling a little to the side, drool forming in the corner of his mouth; though his color is still way way off.

"Elvis," I whisper leaning into him, "I love you."

"Priscilla," he says with his eyes shut tight, "I'm sorry." §

The One

Over the summer months, the profusion of potted philodendron that jammed the window ledges in Ditty's sun porch had turned pale and leggy, now twining pathetically toward the floor. With daylight hours shrinking, and Ditty tired all the time from the pain of her rheumatoid arthritis, she didn't have much inclination to pinch off the trailing stems. Or even give them a drink of water. "Sorry, plants," was the most she could muster.

All week long a young realtor named Rick had been carting people over to see Ditty's house. Yesterday morning when he phoned, he wanted to come by at ten.

"Make it eleven-thirty," she'd told him. Even though the house never got touched in that hour and a half — no dusting, no dragging out the vacuum cleaner to suck up dead brown leaves.

"Mrs. Reynolds," said Rick over the phone, his voice moving into its nasal register, "Mrs. Reynolds, do you really wanna sell your house?"

"Well of course I do," Ditty had snapped, thinking: these young snot-noses have no respect.

Back when they first contemplated buying the place — she and Roger — from a Mrs. Cora Foy — a smile and polite handshake had confirmed the transaction. Nowadays it was all cold business and contracts.

"You stall, you could lose this deal," Rick went on to say.

Deal! Ditty's nose had wrinkled as she held the phone away from her ear. As if that very word *deal* harbored a serious contagion.

"I'll take my chances," she told him setting the phone down firmly in its cradle.

This morning Rick phoned again. He would be coming by soon. He'd given Ditty her marching orders: "Clean up, Mrs. Reynolds, will ya? And take that deer head down off the wall, it grosses people out. And bake something to make the house smell good."

Some nerve! she thought, sliding a tray of raisin cookies out of the stove. They had baked browner than she liked. She probed one with her finger. Still soft. About to stick her own head in the stove, to gauge the heat, the front doorbell rang in a series of musical chimes; stopping a moment to chime all over again.

"Keep your shirt on!" she hollered, the dry stove heat making her cough.

Banging it shut Ditty was thinking that three-hundred-fifty-degrees should bake the same as always. So what caused the cookies to nearly burn? Shaking her head and wiping her hands on her apron, she took her time answering the front door.

On the high brick stoop, just slightly behind Rick, a pretty young woman had on one of those navy-blue pea coats. It reminded Ditty of sailors *on leave* during World War II. A smile played across her lips remembering Roger in his sailor uniform — *sailor suits* they used to call them. Roger — so straight-backed, pressed, eager.

Ditty craned her neck to get a better look at the young woman. Can you afford this place? she was thinking, when Rick announced: "Mrs. Reynolds meet Mrs. Pannatone."

The young woman stepped neatly around the realtor and stuck out her hand. Soft brown leather filling Ditty's palm like warm chocolate. "Glad to meet you," said the young woman with a nice smile.

"Like-wise," said Ditty.

And though the young woman did indeed look quite young in her face, the expression in her green eyes did not. If anything, her eyes looked old.

Too old, Ditty was thinking, feeling something besides arthritis moving through her — a watery sloshy sensation she was unable to pin-point. And though the young woman's eyes rested on Ditty, they seemed focused elsewhere — though nowhere Ditty could make out.

She took her hand back and tucked it into the pocket of her apron. "Well you better come in," she said.

With Rick trailing close behind, the young woman stepped inside Ditty's large foyer.

"Very nice," she said, a brown suede beret set at a jaunty angle on her head. Using both hands, the young woman clutched the beret by its sides, raising it toward the ceiling before bringing it down in front of her in one swift motion — exposing a mound of short, glossy russet-color hair.

At that moment it registered with Ditty that Roger used to remove his fedora that same way when coming in from outdoors. Raising it up like an offering to God she used to think. And thinking it now about the young woman. Whose eyes, Ditty noticed with a start, were the same deep green shade as Roger's eyes.

Rick stepped forward. "We'll show ourselves around, Mrs. Reynolds — if you don't mind." She watched his eyes take in the deer head, still in its spot on the wall by the staircase.

Mind! About to say that she minded very much, instead she wagged a finger. "Be sure and turn off the lights when you leave a room."

"Yeah, yeah, I know all about the lights."

A look, not lost on Ditty, passed from Rick to the young woman. Unbuttoning his smooth black overcoat he said, "Let's start upstairs first, Mrs. Pannatone. If that's okay with you. You see, I like to start high..." And he twirled his arm fast, reminding Ditty of the dark funnel of a tornado.

"Start high," Rick was saying, "working our way down to the basement. Wait till you see the wine cellar! There's space for a thousand bottles."

Ditty crossed her arms over her apron. "Make that fifteen-hundred."

Rick laughed. "Sorry! Fifteen-hundred." And taking the young woman by the elbow, he steered her toward the winding staircase where he announced in a loud voice: "Solid oak!"

As if *you* had anything to do with it, thought Ditty, her eyes narrowing as he rapped on a newel post with his knuckles.

SUSAN TEPPER

"Take care with those steps," she said. "There's thirty-three in all — thirteen up to the first landing, then ten to the short landing, then the last ten steep ones."

Rick laughed again. Ditty wanted to ask what was funny about thirty-three steps, when the young woman lifted her head and sniffed. "Ummm. Something smells delicious."

"After you're finished with your looking you can come to the kitchen for raisin cookies."

The young woman glanced in the direction of the sweet aroma.

"That's right," said Ditty. "Kitchen's just around that bend. You'll like it. It's big. Got a wood-burning oven in the wall."

"And a stove!" Rick added.

"Well naturally there's a stove!" Rolling her eyes, Ditty looked toward the young woman, saying, "Roger — he was my husband — Roger had that oven built there to bake bread."

Standing quite still, Ditty was picturing the plump round yeast batters, in bowls draped with kitchen towels, set on the windowsills to rise overnight. Back then the kitchen always felt warm. Too warm. Steam fogging the windows. She'd have to yank off her sweater, fan herself with a towel. Raw yeast smelling to her like something that got coughed up from deep inside some animal like a lamb.

Roger had been serious about his baking. Tearing open packets of BREWER YEAST, to sprinkle in bowls filled with water, while Ditty played the radio and danced around the kitchen in her bra — god but she could dance in those days!

Roger was a serious man. Freshly baked bread had been a serious matter. There were no children. They'd tried and tried.

Shall we? Ditty heard him saying.

Shall we? She stood in the foyer swaying to faraway music. Shall we?

"Mrs. Reynolds? Mrs. Reynolds? Hello?"

Ditty blinked. Next to the staircase, still clutching the beret, the young woman was looking at her. Not in any rude or curious way — just a friendly sort of looking.

Ditty coughed then, clearing her throat. "What did you say your full name was?"

"Rose Pannatone."

"Rose Pannatone," repeated Ditty softly.

88

In the center of the foyer, roses in three hues of pink wove through the round fringed rug.

"What kind of name is that?" she asked the young woman.

"Italian."

"Well you might want to make pizza in the oven. It's brick-lined."

Rick spoke up then, in none too nice a voice. "Hey, Mrs. Reynolds! You're spoiling my whole tour. You're giving away all the fine points of the house. Mrs. Pannatone won't have any surprises, you're telling her everything before she even gets there."

"Do you have a problem with that — Mrs. Panna... Panna..." Ditty stood there blinking. "I don't understand. I said it just fine a minute ago. Now it seems to have gotten stuck in my throat." She coughed again.

"It's Pannatone," said the young woman, smiling. "And I really don't mind you telling me about the house, it doesn't matter. I mean, I'll find out anyway, won't I? One way or another."

Ditty bent over to blow dust off the stepped, mahogany telephone table. Then she stood up straight. Looking in the direction of the young woman, their eyes locking. Something stirring in Ditty. Something having to do with time, and things shared; things of a secretive nature.

"Mrs. Pannatone," she said, this time pronouncing it perfectly. She moved toward the staircase where she stood close to the young woman. And Ditty started to reach out, to touch the sleeve of the pea coat, then thought otherwise. Strong winter sunlight, shooting through spoked glass from the sunburst window over the front door, seemed to set the russet hair on fire.

Her next words Ditty chose with care. "If you buy this house, and come to live in it, you won't find out anything you don't already know."

"Like that deer," Rick muttered.

"It came with the house," said Ditty.

"That's right." The young woman nodding agreeably. And using both hands she set the brown suede beret back on her head.

Don't do that! Ditty almost screamed, her own hands flying to her heart; as if the russet hair were a candle, the beret snuffing out its final glow.

The young woman took no notice of Ditty's distress. With eyes newly shimmering like green glass, she said, "I won't need to look any further. This is the one." §

The Velvet Box

When Uncle Sloppy wouldn't stop crying after about a week, my cousin Pete, who is seven, placed a tiny velvet music box in the old man's mouth. It was red and soft and squishy like a velvet tomato, with little rows of seed pearls sewn on. It belonged to my mother, and when I first saw it, I naturally took it to be a pin cushion.

My younger sister Bibi said that Uncle would choke and die on the pearls. I stared at him and thought if he died it would be a blessing. He hadn't moved a finger or a toe in more than a year since the roof of his house caved in. My mother sometimes said: *a simple roof repair...* but then her voice trailed off and she looked sad. He'd always been in this mess or that, which is how come they nicknamed him Sloppy. I had just started the sixth grade, after they brought Uncle here; and had a hard time concentrating on math, my worst subject.

He lay flat out in a bed they dragged onto our enclosed back porch, staying perfectly still with his mouth flung open. Pete said Uncle was like a stick of butter. The only thing that moved on Uncle were his tears.

As we stood around his bed, the velvet music box began playing the theme song from MIGHTY JOE YOUNG.

91

"What the...?" said Bibi her brown eyes wide and gaping.

"He must have bit down on his own!" I yelled. We three inched closer to the bed.

"If he bit down then it's a miracle," said Bibi.

"Like with Jesus?" Pete wanted to know.

"Yeah, sorta something like that," I answered shushing him.

These days I wasn't giving Jesus too much credit. Not since the priest made everyone stand up in church and say *the pledge*. All the grownups stood up and swore to God they wouldn't read any dirty books or watch dirty movies. The priest called them *banned by the church* but I knew what he had in mind.

We three didn't stand up. Nobody looked our way. Probably they figured it didn't matter, that we were just bored kids not paying attention.

I felt proud that day. I had whispered to Bibi and Pete to stay down, and they usually listened, so we all stayed down in the pew. It didn't feel right, that old priest deciding which books and movies. I had wondered when the last time was he'd been to see a movie. I figured a lot of the men would sneak off, anyway, when their wives were busy cleaning the house or at the supermarket. Maybe even a few of the women, too. My own dear mother had PEYTON PLACE buried deep in her underwear drawer. I found it accidentally when I went searching for safety pins to hold our kite together. I had heard her say PEYTON PLACE to my aunt Cecile, then the both of them giggled.

***

The soft velvet box in Uncle's mouth played BEAUTI-FUL DREAMER. Uncle seemed to calm down. Or maybe it was just shock, hearing sounds coming out of his mouth after all this time. It didn't much matter. That same pretty music had calmed down MIGHTY JOE YOUNG. I loved the way the big ape twirled 'round and 'round to the music.

"Watch out, you're stepping on his tube," Bibi said to Pete.

Pete's habit of tripping over things, or sitting on stuff and breaking them was getting out of control. Last week he sat on my mother's favorite LP record of Patty Page singing the sand dune song. Then, the other day, he tripped and disconnected one of Uncle's wires. It must've been an important wire because Uncle started to turn a funny color, then his eyes rolled back in his head and my mother had to phone the doctor to get him reconnected. Afterwards she was very angry. She said if we couldn't be more careful she'd have to ban us from visiting Uncle's room.

"This is all your fault," Bibi had yelled at Pete near the garage. He'd hung his head looking ashamed, so we three made a pow-wow to forgive him. Pete loved Uncle more than anything. Before the roof, when Uncle was still himself, he used to bounce Pete on his knee and call him *little sonny boy.* Pete missed that; he missed Uncle more than all of us combined.

"All right, all right, stop your sniveling," I'd told him.

Pete had wiped his nose and stood before the garage looking at me like a dog waiting for the next command.

Growing bored with the velvet music box, I said, "Let's go get some ice cream."

BUNGALOW BAR truck had just hit our street and was ringing its bell.

"Do you think it's OK leaving the box with Uncle?" Bibi sounded worried.

Halfway out of the room, I turned to look back at him. The song had played itself three or four times now. "He's fine. Leave it with him, I think it makes him feel better."

When Bibi got worried he squeezed her eyes under long dark bangs. She was doing it now. "What if he chokes on the little pearls while we're getting our ice cream?"

"Then it'll be God's will."

"How can you say that Henrietta?"

"Look, I want a toasted almond bar." I pinched my sister's arm and she jabbed me back. It was a sweltering day. If I didn't get my toasted almond bar, I couldn't predict what might happen. "C'mon, we have to hurry or the ice cream man will think we're not coming."

Pete pushed past me speeding down the hallway. I ran behind him listening to the truck bell sounding weaker, like it was pulling away. Sure enough, outside, the ice cream truck was already three houses past ours. We had to run fast to catch up.

"*Stoooooooooop!*" I screamed over the ringing. It stopped in front of the Malone house, the four Malone children quickly surrounding the truck window. I felt panicked. I kept running toward it sweat rolling down my face. Those Malones might buy up all the toasted almond bars. Because once they'd found out I liked them best, they decided toasted almond was their favorite, too.

My mother only allowed us one ice cream each. The

Malone children were allowed two, and their mother bought bags and bags of cookies and candy and potato chips and big cartons of soda they stored in the garage.

I stood there fidgety waiting my turn. I watched each Malone get two toasted almond bars a piece. Debbie Malone took a bite grinning at me with ice cream on her chin. The bars today looked especially golden toasted.

That's 8 gone already, I was calculating. And that's not counting other streets where kids had already gotten their ice cream. Suddenly I felt miserable. Those damn Malones and all their candy in their magical candy house. And they beat us to the truck. Bibi and Pete looked envious, too.

Finally it was our turn and there were enough left. "It's a total miracle," I said, giving those Malones a mean look.

The Malone house was small like ours, identical to ours and all the others on our block, and the surrounding blocks. Most of the fathers on our block had been in World War 2. I don't think Mr. Malone served. Besides all the sweets in their house, it was the only house with a huge tree out front, that made caterpillar nests in the summer, and horrible black hairy caterpillars that crawled all over the place. The sidewalk always had hundreds of squashed ones. My mother said that Mr. Malone went out at night and stepped on the caterpillars. I had once seen him chain their dog to the basement post, whipping the poor beast almost to death. He was a thin man with dark greasy hair. My mother had said he was *wiry*, and that she didn't trust wiry men. I wasn't afraid of him. He beat the dog but mostly acted nice toward us kids.

Time and again we were warned to stay out of the Malone house. But then my mother would get busy with Uncle, and we would get that urge for sweets and go knocking on their back door. Mary Malone was the youngest, a skinny girl with a face like a bird who had no problem sharing. Her sisters, older and fatter, only gave out one cookie at a time. They watched you eat it, then whispered among themselves about whether to give you another. The older sisters never shared the candy. Never. They stood in front of that candy cabinet like guards.

After we finished off the toasted almond bars, we wandered toward our house. Bibi and I sat on the grass. Pete climbed onto the back of a plastic lawn deer yelling *giddyup* and slapping its rump, though it was forbidden to ride them. He said he was going to get a rifle and blast through the Malone candy cabinet.

"Well that's really dumb," said Bibi. "Don't you think you'll wreck all the candy? Don't you think you'll blast it to bits?" He looked surprised toppling the deer over and landing on the grass. He said he didn't want any of their damn candy anyway.

"We'll get our own," I told them. "And you better put that back up before my mother sees and has a fit."

"We don't have any money," Pete said standing it up next to the other two deer.

"Uncle does. Uncle has money in a bunch of socks," I said. "Look, that deer is cockeyed, it's not straight anymore, you dented its nose."

"Are you making this up about the socks, Henrietta?" My sister looked doubtful about Uncle having any money. She squatted in the grass pulling out dandelions. "If he has money, then why is he living here with us? Why isn't he in the Shady Rest Home getting better? Mom said he's here because he's got no money."

I laughed loudly, jumping up and running toward the house. Inside, I could hear BEAUTIFUL DREAMER coming from the back porch. I went there, gave Uncle a wave, then sat on the windowsill pushing up the screen and dangling my legs outside. Big purple hydrangeas bloomed near the downspout.

"Uncle you have hydrangeas growing out your window," I said not looking at him. There wasn't much you could say to him these days. There wasn't much to say to anyone who couldn't answer you back. BEAUTIFUL DREAMER had stopped. But then he must've bit down again because it started playing.

"That song you're playing is called BEAUTIFUL DREAMER," I told him despite his not being able to answer. I tilted my head back listening to the music play itself out. It made me feel calm, too.

Pete came in, then Bibi. "His eyes are closed," my sister said.

"He's dreaming. A beautiful dream." I smiled. "We made Uncle feel peaceful. We have every right to be proud."

"Henrietta! Bibi!" Mother was shouting our names and rushing toward his bed. She pulled the velvet box out of Uncle's mouth, placing her ear against his chest. Finally she straightened up.

Looking at the three of us she said, "He's not breathing."

Stunned, we stared back at her. The little red velvet music box sat quietly on her palm.

"We'll never talk about this," she said. "Not a single word." Then she left the porch, and us alone with Uncle. §

About the Author

P rior to settling down and studying writing at NYU and New School University, Susan Tepper was an actress, flight attendant, marketing manager, bank teller, interior decorator, travel agent, singer, tour director and rescue worker. The late David Kozubei (founder of David's Books in Ann Arbor) once told her that she has lived the writer's life.